MAGPIES

Books by Lynne Barrett

Fiction

The Land of Go
The Secret Names of Women
Magpies

As Editor

The James M. Cain Cookbook
(with Roy Hoopes)

Birth: A Literary Companion
(with Kristin Kovacic)

MAGPIES

By Lynne Barrett

Carnegie Mellon University Press
Pittsburgh 2011

ACKNOWLEDGMENTS

My thanks to the publications where the following stories previously appeared, in slightly different form: "Links" in *Painted Bride Quarterly*; "One Hippopotamus" as "One Mississippi" in *Apalachee Review*; "The Noir Boudoir" in *Miami Noir*, Akashic Books; "Gift Wrap" in the *Sun-Sentinel*, republished in *A Dixie Christmas*, Algonquin Books, and *Irrepressible Appetites*, Rock Press; "When, He Wondered" in *Ellery Queen's Mystery Magazine*; and "Texaco on Biscayne" in *Saw Palm*.

This book was completed with a fellowship from the Florida Division of Cultural Affairs.

Book design: James Berndt

Library of Congress Control Number 2011926143
ISBN 978-0-88748-543-5

10 9 8 7 6 5 4 3 2 1

for James

CONTENTS

Links

"Language this," Avery said, the first day I worked at eBright-lights.com. Worked there, worded there. At my blank look, he said, "It doesn't need much, just some polishing up, a couple of sweet phrases, you know. That's your specialty, right?"

Even as I nodded he was turning away, my new boss, a high-speed guy with short dark hair, a techno shirt woven in tiny blue-gray waffles. He made his way, stopping to offer a word or smile at other desks, to his corner of the big room we all shared. This was a democratic place, I'd been told already. The two founders, Avery and Thad, were 28, but that was part of their authority, their sheer youth, their lack of formality. They exhaled <u>Success</u>.

So I set to work—occasionally, furtively, using paper to make notes. *The Stylus*, the magazine where I'd worked for the past eight years, my whole career, had folded. After operating at an honorable loss for over a century, the intellectual bauble of one rich man after another, *The Stylus* vanished and with it my toehold in New York literary life. My friend since high school, Celie, had been trying to get me to quit, pointing out that in this boom even temps were making 30K while I was accepting so much less, stuck (her term) living in New Jersey with my brother. But I'd hung on, imagining myself to be climbing as I went from doing captions to listings of literary events to (unsigned) short reviews, plus editing the works of the regular contributors, many of them survivors from the '50s who turned in pages with type so pale you imagined their old ribbons on one final round of being hit hard by Smith-Corona keys.

So I should have been grateful when the last owner was unable to snag another taker and let *The Stylus* sink. Articles appeared in tribute to Peter Alphonse Delisle, the hearty madman who'd been editor for the past 46 years, discoverer of geniuses he launched but rarely paid. The articles lamented the passing of an era, Delisle gone like other landmarks, but no one cared. Within a week, I was whisked into Silicon Alley's warren by Celie and allowed to begin at a salary so rich my head spun, at eBrightlights. com. We covered "the evening's things to do, with links to buy sport & concert tix at discounts & deals at restaurants," in sixteen cities with others clamoring to be listed.

They gave me a slick laptop. I lifted it, doubting it really had anything inside, but when I commanded it to print, the printer chirped and produced. Wires crawled to my desk through holes in the exposed brick walls, and light streamed in through the arched tops of the tall windows of this 1800s building. It looked like the place where Bartleby scrivened. And this was what scrivening had come to.

My first task was a piece on megaplexes submitted by some teenage content provider out there, his writing rambling and misspelled. I fixed, I ordered, I made it flow. I e-mailed it across the room.

Avery walked over and stood beside my chair. "What is this, Mary Louise?" he said. He held his laptop, displaying my article, 500 words, clear and coherent.

"No, no," he said. "You don't want this. You have to blow it up. Spider your story. No one can read more than a paragraph anymore. Don't make it linear. Forget linearity. You want to jump 'em to a different page." And he showed me how he wanted it fragmented, how to pick a phrase to hit, to make you leap off to get more info.

"Will anyone ever read the whole thing, then?"

"Who knows? Who cares? People don't have time to plow through some long, dragged-out report—they want to be able to skip to just what interests them. That's how the mind really works," he said.

"Whose mind?"

"The modern mind. The web mind. Anyway we *want* them to hop around, because each page carries advertising. See, that's the goal, to get the eyeballs on as many pages as possible. There's no preferred order. The pages are all equal in cyberspace."

"Why do they call them pages, then?"

"Reverence for antiquity," Avery said, and shot me a look. He had large dark eyes, with thick eyelashes, I couldn't help but notice.

"Ah," I said, and went on to language some more.

I learned how to do it swiftly, to think in target, and link. I may be a Luddite but if I'm going to learn a technology, I'll learn it right.

My Chair

It cost $700. Violet gray, ergonomically correct, so comfy I kept catching myself making a nestling motion, rocking my butt. The seat was so wide I could sit in it cross-legged. There were ten of them in the room, the lowliest employee, me, seated as well as the Chief Operations Officer (Avery) and the CEO (Thad).

The fabric was synthetic velvet, soft and indestructible. The paint on the arms and base had the depth and luster of a new Italian car. The casters had been developed by NASA. Later, the chairs were cited as a sign of Avery's extravagance, in the article in the *Wall Street Journal*, but actually Thad picked them.

Success

That first day—March 13, 2000—the stock hit 36 ¾, a new high, and Thad and Avery ordered in a spread from Hispanasia, lobster spring rolls with a chipotle dipping sauce, delicious little arepas, and amazing wasabi sorbet. If I worked there six months, I'd have options on a bit of stock myself. I rode the train home to New Jersey with a pleasant burn in my mouth, strange hopes.

The Stock

On the day I started, Thad and Avery were worth $6 million each. On paper.

Celie had described to me the period of the IPO, in February, when Thad and Avery went out, along with the Chief Financial Officer, an old guy who'd worked for Thad's dad on Wall Street, to whip up the investors. Thad knew venture capitalists and had the social connections, while Avery was the idea man, the one who understood technology. They'd been roommates together at Wharton, but they'd quit to do this. Quitting B-school was itself considered a credential in the economy of dreams.

Just before the IPO, Thad took Celie out on a $3,000 date (of course paid for by eBrightlights.com) with a reporter along, and this was written up in the *Times*' Styles section in a piece quivering with envious snark. On the strength of it, the bankers raised the initial offering price by $2, to $18. The day of the IPO the stock went to $28 ⅜, the following day to $32.

Under the friends and family clause, Celie was allowed to buy a bit of the stock in advance at the IPO price. She sold it fast and made her little sum. She was cagey about how much. She'd cashed out ahead of the peak, but she felt happy to have her safe pot in the bank. She sold ads at a better established dot com, and she often said these later startups wouldn't last. She also got to keep from the date the little tissuey Tuleh dress she'd worn, which hadn't even figured into the total reported in the paper. She and Thad were broken up within a month—after a $3,000 date, she said, the usual ones are just plain drinking—but stayed friends.

Thad and Avery were only theoretical millionaires. They couldn't sell their shares for 180 days, by law, and even then, really, they wouldn't be able to sell too much without indicating they'd lost confidence in their venture, which would sink the value. They had, as well, the millions the IPO had raised, but that had to be spent on building the company. They were hiring a sales force and planning offices in Miami and L.A. Sometimes I'd visualize all of us as pumping one of those early attempts at a plane, just a winged bicycle, something that can't fly, but somehow, just for a moment, through faith and frantic effort, hovers.

In April, though, the stock went down. The whole NASDAQ took a hit. There was mention of belt tightening, but all we could do was grow.

There was a bad day in May when we dropped below the IPO price, and Avery went around whistling, talking people up. Absolute confidence was necessary to float us. Thad had a hangover, Avery whispered, leave him alone. He's just such a party guy. Thad was sitting at his desk, throwing darts at a newspaper cutout of Allan Greenspan's face. The next day, the stock was back up. But not as high as it had been in March. And it went on like that, into the summer of the cows.

The Summer of the Cows

Silly plaster cows were stuck all over New York, painted by artists according to different themes. There was even one in New Jersey by Pal's Cabin, the restaurant that had grown from a little 1930s hot dog stand, not far from our house in West Orange. eBrightlights.com lost some workers, people who jumped to other ventures. Thad's dad was said to have cashed out, though Thad denied it. But we still had eyeballs. We sold lots of tickets, losing money on many of them, but we had to do that to get market share. And we had market share, supposedly, hordes of kids with disposable income searching for things to do. Backers came into the office and spoke to the boys at length, before investing more.

And I was more necessary than before. I could take a piece and rewrite it to localize it for every city we covered. I was part of the demand for content. The demand for profit. Damned demand. I started working Saturdays, which Avery had been doing all along. Thad spent his weekends in the Hamptons, going to investors' parties.

One hot Saturday afternoon, Avery invited me out to eat at a place he liked, Judy's Sushi. For us to share, he ordered what he called the Dynamite Pleasure Blob, smoked eel on California rolls with some extra rich soy sauce, almost soy syrup, drizzled over it. I noticed on the little wine promotion tent on the table, the typo: "Spakling wines."

"See this?" I said, laughing.

"You do that a lot?"

"What?"

"Random proofreading."

"I guess," I said. "There are mistakes everywhere. On bill-boards even."

"Aggravating?"

"Sometimes. Or amusing. Why?"

"Uh-huh," he said. "I suspected it. <u>Attention Surplus Disorder</u>."

"Oh dear," I said. "What are the symptoms?"

"You can sit still for hours on end, working on something. I've seen that. You probably read whole books—"

"Well, once I've begun—"

"At a sitting—"

"When I get the chance—"

"Focus through distraction? Don't need to get up and move? Keep on through interruptions, delays, sidetracks? Classic case: <u>Attention Surplus Disorder</u>. Principally afflicts women."

"Afflicts?"

"Sure. You're stuck, Mary Louise. It's old thinking. It's well known that we guys with A.D.D. are the ones who are truly creative. My mind just bops from one thing to another. I have rapid ideation. Aren't you jealous?"

I couldn't help but laugh at him. "Well, what do they prescribe for my disorder?"

"Wine," he said, "and sex."

And so, yes, mmhmm, I did go home with him. That one time I saw the place he and Thad shared—on Grand Street, a studio cut out of what must have once been a big old apartment with plaster doodads stuck to the high ceiling. It was horribly hot and stark, just beds and computers, really. I knew it would rent for more than I could bear to imagine. We had the bottle of "spakling" wine, Italian champagne, quite good I thought, and inexpensive.

Avery described to me the places he'd looked at that he could theoretically afford someday, Upper East Side apartments with butlers' pantries. It was six months since the IPO, the stock down to 9 ½, but still worth something. On schedule, the investment bankers were cashing them in for a little, but they'd get nothing like what there'd have been at one time. Still, he was certain all would be well. The gloomy business guys in the *New York Observer* were always going on about a bubble and the scent of tulips and all, but they were old and didn't understand what was happening with the Internet. "This is the Union Pacific Railroad," he said. "This is the telegraph and the Atlantic Cable, this is <u>STEAM</u> for God's sake."

We sat on his bed with our feet out the window to catch a breeze. Me and the barefoot theoretical millionaire. The city outside was hushed, for once, so I imagined it holding its breath. Everyone was waiting for his kiss. We had sex and then we went outside for a while to let our sweat evaporate. When it got dark we finished the white wine and entangled our bodies again.

Sleeping, he trembled like a dog.

Attention Surplus Disorder

I can't close a book once I start. Well, except when there's a dangling modifier on the first page or something like that. That lets me stop. But otherwise I forge on even when I can tell how it's going to come out.

Yes, I confess. I got through *Bleak House.* I can keep track of Russian characters with triple names.

And I can't stop reading the world. Each day, on my way to the train, I pause to be amused at the signs perpetually hanging one above the other in the window of an old pharmacy near the station:

Blood Glucose Monitors

Whitman Samplers.

I collect errors in its/it's. Few know which is which anymore. I've even more than once seen her's. The apostrophe—people just take a stab at it these days, like a ritual that's lost its meaning. Apostrophes meander with no relation to possession or contraction—indeed often they flourish over plurals, decorative and useless. I have elaborated a secret theory that this reflects our relationships, our confusion about whether, no matter how many connections we proliferate, we can ever count on belonging to each other.

Continuity may be humdrum, but I can't let go of it. Can't drop anyone from my Christmas card list. Can't stop listening to Celie complaining about her boyfriend though she's had the same complaints about one boyfriend or another for the past eight years. Can't help but assume, when I've slept with someone, that when I've gone home the next day, and on some level ever after, we'll be connected. In some way.

Attention is love. I believe that.

Our House in West Orange

The house my brother and I share—bought, thank God, by my grandparents before World War II—is an ugly brick two bedroom on a steep road with, coming off that, a near vertical driveway that rises between cement walls into a garage so small it's a major feat to get a car into it unscratched. The place is a geometry experiment, so many acute angles. We thrifty people who own our however-many cubic feet of New Jersey are both tempted to sell at some huge price to the city people before they wise up and terrified that we'll never get our hands on anything like it again.

While real estate boomed, in the late '80s, then dropped and boomed again, my grandmother Sottile, who we called Granny Lou, lived on there, much too spry to quit it despite my father's pleas that she move to an assisted living place near him and Mom out in Boonton. Granny Lou survived—bitching, always, about the taxes—with the house ever more ramshackle but gaining value.

My older brother Barry (for more on him, go to My Brother) lived with her. For security, that was the explanation, but in truth they were very close. When Granny Lou fell in the back yard (which, despite much clean fill, still tilted at a 40 degree angle away from the garage) and had to have her hip replaced, my brother waited on her tenderly. Granny Lou died of pneumonia that winter, but Barry and I think she just gave up once she had the hip replacement, when she looked at the terrain she'd have to relearn to negotiate. At that point I'd survived two years with Celie, sharing a tiny place with a metal door thick as the one on a bank vault, over in Brooklyn. As Celie moved up to Manhattan, I couldn't follow, on my *Stylus* wages, so I joined my brother, enchanted with the idea of a real living room.

My father threatens to sell, but he's willing to wait. In theory, Barry and I are fixing the place up, but of course, we don't want to move when we are so thriftily housed. The property taxes, Granny Lou's bane, are cheaper than any rent we could hope to find.

My brother has the room that was, once upon a time, our father's, with Dad's old felt college football banners on the walls. I have the attic, the garret, Granny Lou called it, with ceilings that slant down to the knee walls, and one dormer in the front. It's cozy up there, where the house's many angles meet. Neither of us wants to take over Granny Lou's room, so we call it the guest room and leave it as is, with its white chenille bedspread and wedding photo of our grandparents on the dresser.

The house has a permanent smell of cream of tomato soup. On the couch, on every chair, there's an afghan or shawl. I knit them. I'm in love with beautiful yarns, still full of lanolin, hand-dyed in colors that warm you just to touch them, fuchsia, pimiento. I knit in the evenings in our living room. It has bookcases with glass doors, on either side of the fireplace, filled with bestsellers of the '50s, Anya Seton and Francis Parkinson Keyes, and triple anthologies of mysteries with a freckling of mildew. Sometimes while I knit I watch old movies where Cary Grant, millionaire businessman, drops everything in ardent pursuit of Doris Day or Ingrid Bergman. I have to wonder whether everyone knew this to be a fiction at the time, or whether sometime between then and now men changed. Because no one pursues women like that anymore. And in case you think I'm not the type, even my most beautiful friends, like Celie, say so. Men approach us—no, they don't even approach—they simply allow themselves to be in our vicinity, exhibiting a mixture of fear and disdain. They never say what they want. Instead, at some point, often so late at night that we're too tired to care anymore, we lurch together. And next day they panic.

If you don't work together, of course, they can simply avoid you, not call, vanish. But Avery and I shared the office, that one big democratic room. That Sunday morning in August, he'd kissed me but said nothing significant before I left his apartment to take the train home. Thad had come in and was watching TV, and that obviously constrained us, but I had a bad feeling. On that Monday, when I arrived at work, I took Avery in—the shiny white-purple under his eyes, like the insides of mussel shells, his hair glossy black, the blue veins of his arms—I was <u>paying attention</u>, and I could see the panic. The man's mouth was dry, I could tell it across the room. I knew what I had to do. Nothing. Just be completely normal, or, okay, a little less in touch than usual. No bright little e-mails, no initiating conversations, just keeping it low key till he realized I wasn't expecting a thing. That night I went home and launched into my well-practiced <u>post-man cure</u>.

Post-man Cure

My system requires bringing home a batch of Evening Star lilies from Fresh Fields, some ciabatta and roast garlic spread. Roast garlic floods my body with goodwill and the flowers decadently scent my room till they drive out memory. Then I play, obsessively, certain '80s music. I believe I imprinted on it in high school, after my first disappointment (a guy who, no kidding, was named Jean-Loup), so that I need it when the dopamine of sex has left my body. I recommend the Motels' "Total Control." Or something by The Impersonators. (Stream <u>MeetTheImpersonatorsVanGogh-aGoGosample.mp3</u>)

> *Used to go*
> *with Edgar Allan Poe*
> *but I left him for*
> *Vincent Van Gogh*
> *I been dating*
> *Dostoevsky*
> *I been kissing*
> *kissing Picasso*
> *All the boys I pick*
> *are peculiar*
> *Can't understand*
> *why I like them so*
> *They like to suffer—oh!*
> *Van Gogh a Go Go*
> *And they've got ego-go-go-go-go-go-go-go!*
> *Van Gogh a Go Go*

After a week or so, the panic flutter had died down, and Avery and I were back to normal, as if we'd never had that Dynamite Pleasure Blob evening. In September, when I'd been there six months, he gave me my stock options. And promoted me. Officially, I was Editor in Chief. No raise, though. Things were a little tight, he said, but the stock options would make up for that, eventually. They were cutting the work force by 22 percent. We'd be lean and nimble and headed for a great fourth quarter. Talking at his desk, figuring ways to update the site less often but keep the home page fresh, we were all business.

And yet, I did feel our night should count, that we were connected. I suppose that's why, as so many others left, I didn't. Though, remember, I didn't leave *The Stylus* either. It disappeared on me.

The Stylus

As an editor, Edgar Allan Poe was known as "the Slasher" for his witty, merciless reviews. He drew readers to *Burton's Gentleman's Magazine*, *Graham's Magazine*, the *Southern Literary Messenger*, magazines he built, while he, barely paid by the publishers, became bitter and mouthed off when drunk till he was fired. By the mid-1840s, impoverished and famous, Poe yearned to be his own boss. At least twice, he circulated the prospectus for a magazine of his own, called *The Stylus*, but he never received enough backing. He was still hoping to launch it when he died in Baltimore after his own especially bad night on the town.

Poe was reviled in an obituary by Rufus Griswold, whose work Poe happened to have slashed all too accurately in reviews. One imagines Poe would view Griswold's then becoming his literary executor (a position he bought by paying off Poe's aunt) as some sort of macabre joke. While denouncing Poe as dissolute, Griswold profited by reissuing his works. As the century progressed, Stevenson, Conan Doyle, Melville, Wilde, Conrad and others stole from, excuse me, were inspired by him.

In 1899, the literati of New York City threw a banquet in Poe's honor to recognize his genius, according to Peter Alphonse Delisle, retired *Stylus* editor, whom I visited now and then in the summer and fall. He was living with his daughter in Montclair. I usually took him some flowers or fruit or a book. I know, I know, he hadn't treated me all that well, but he was an old man, and we'd worked together for years. I couldn't abandon him. He sat with his bad leg up—Peter Alphonse Delisle had that very literary ailment, gout—and held forth. Around him cartons overflowed with the early records of *The Stylus*, whose history he said he was writing. He read me letters from literary luminaries of the twentieth century, most of them begging to be paid for their contributions. He told me how, after the 1899 banquet, one Richard Pentreath Hodges, a Poe devotee, obtained the backing of a railroad tycoon turned philanthropist and began *The Stylus*, with its tradition of editors who use their middle names.

Of course you've noticed the connection between my comfort anthem by The Impersonators and *The Stylus*. It's possible that Poe was enough to get me to sign up for eight years of low pay, I'll concede. I've always had a thing for him.

My Brother

My brother hates waste. Barry can squeeze a quarter till the eagle screams, Granny Lou used to say, proudly.

For the past thirteen years, Barry has been a substitute teacher in various Essex County schools. Barry is a large man and a patient one, and nothing the students do frightens him, so he is much in demand. But he has never wanted to move up and teach. The money he gets is enough for him to nurture his hobby. Barry collects old products, in their original packaging. When he was still in college, he developed a sideline, coming in after estate sales, getting paid to haul away all that remained in the kitchen and basement. Some things he sold at flea markets, and what didn't sell he donated to charity for a tax deduction. But Barry kept the old boxes of Jell-O and Durkee spice tins, bygone comestibles, before others saw them as objects of value. He built his collection, trading with others who specialized in the effluvia left behind by business on its march. It was a natural next step for him to get on eBay, and he's done well there. For my birthday and Christmas he gives me perfect old perfume bottles, from My Sin to Joy; I have quite a display on the blue mirror tray on my dresser. Barry has put together, in our basement, a complete old time soda fountain he pulled out of a building in Newark, and now he's slowly stocking it. Really, there's no way our dad is ever going to get him out of Granny Lou's house.

In his trading, my brother wound up with two old cars, beaters he calls them, simple dented late '80s sedans. I take whichever is at the bottom of the driveway in the morning over to the South Orange station, and drive it home at night. Barry by no means lacks generosity. He shares his cars with me, and often he takes bags of clothes into school, things he's rounded up after house sales, sweat pants and jeans and so on, and gives them away. He says a lot of poor kids skip school simply because they don't have anything decent to wear. As I mentioned, he hates waste.

Paying Attention

In November, the morning light angling into the office hit the dusty folds of Avery's corduroy pants and his metallic whiskers. He hadn't shaved. I was certain he'd been there overnight, but I didn't mention it.

Thad was unable to wring any more money out of the backers. Thad's dad was seen on *Wall Street Week* speaking of the virtues of bricks and mortar.

Early in December, Celie was laid off. From her supposedly secure, much bigger company. She had her eBrightlights IPO nest egg to live on, and unemployment, and told me she was out there vigorously finding something else, working her address book. She urged me to do the same before my job disappeared.

Others followed this kind of advice. As the staff drifted away, I kept working long hours, but no matter how early I came in, how late I left, Avery was there, working. We were intense, tired, neurons firing. Did you know that nerves have their own little exterior skeletons? Your head's full of primitive creatures. As I got less sleep, I noticed the worsening of a symptom I have always had, seeing, when I read a word, the other words it can twist into. I found myself proofreading to make sure none of these had slipped by me.

Before Christmas, Avery told me to stop coming in on Saturdays, since we were reusing content more. Our site still had ads, but their quality had declined, from national companies to local ones.

On January 18th, a survey I'd written ("Where Do You Go Out After a Break-Up?") was still featured on our home page, after two weeks. This was a new low. I looked at the site's dancing figures and hot colors, its blue connections, and knew it false.

I hit the survey link, went to the b-board. There hadn't been many responses. Above them, I noticed the banner from a hardware warehouse: Free Stud Finder. I had to laugh.

Three days later, on a Sunday, from home, I checked the site to see if my survey had drawn further hits. And I got:

Error 404. Not found. Please recheck URL and try again.

I drove like crazy to the station. On the way, I coated my throat, lips, and nose with Vaseline, entering winter like a channel swimmer. Over my head I pulled a mohair smoke ring I had knitted. I stood up on the platform, waiting for the 12:02 in a wicked wind. As I pulled myself onto the train, I caught a glimpse of my reflected silhouette, in boots, long coat, shawl, and cowl, a lady outline from a hundred years ago. I could imagine that somehow time had spun back, undoing so much technology. The train was nearly empty as we crossed New Jersey towards the Manhattan skyline, a shadow insubstantial as chiffon against the tin sky. When I came out of Penn Station, I was hit with a spatter of freezing rain.

Other parts of the building hummed, but on our floor it was quiet. I got inside to find Avery in the dark, curled up in his comfy seat, gray in the gray light, with his parka over him.

"What's going on?" I said. "The site's down."

"They cut us off," he said.

"Who?"

"The server. We couldn't pay them. And the creditors want their money, and nobody'll lend us anything. I can't even pay the electric bill."

"Where's Thad?"

"Thad moved back in with Daddy. We sublet the apartment a while back. I, uh—" He gave a sigh of such exhaustion, I could hear his lungs shake. "I've been living here," he said.

"I knew it," I said.

"Should have done it sooner."

"When did you eat last?"

He just looked at me. Such thick lashes.

"You're fired," he said. "I guess. I mean, me too. We're broke. The shares are worthless, and we have so much debt." He smiled sweetly. "It's a relief to admit it."

And so—what else?—I took him <u>home</u>.

I called Barry and he drove into the city, weather and all. While we waited for him, Avery gathered the clothes he'd stashed in the empty desks. On Avery's advice, we took his laptop and my own. I gathered my papers into a trash can and carried them out that way. Barry wanted to rescue <u>my chair</u>. I'd told him how much I liked it. He fit two into his trunk, padding them with Avery's towels. He couldn't close the trunk, but used a bungee, taking care to make it all secure. "The vultures will be here any minute," Avery said. He said it several times.

Home

Cyclamen whistled pink in the window. I'll never forget how Avery looked, in all his pallid New York weariness, sitting in Granny Lou's '50s kitchen with its rose and gray wallpaper and, on the scalloped shelves, some of Barry's finest vintage products on display, the Ipana toothpaste, the Royal Baking Powder, the furniture polish named Pride. Avery gazed around, at me, at Barry, at our little house, and in truth I was braced for some scorn, but he said, "I've stuck my parents with a second mortgage," and put his head down. I thought he was crying and dreaded how he was going to feel next day, to know I'd seen that, but he simply went to sleep. Barry carried him into the living room and put him on the couch, and I covered him with an afghan.

I crept down once in the night to check, but he hadn't moved.

He slept into Monday. In the morning, I went out and bought roast garlic and ciabatta and the *Times*. When Avery got up and showered, that afternoon, Barry had just come home from a day with the fourth grade. We made a fire in the fireplace, and shared the bread and garlic and had pasta with some veal and roasted peppers Mom had frozen for us last week. Avery ate a lot and said little, just sat looking at the firelight on all the books and Granny Lou's bill-paying desk. We read the brief piece in the *Times* about the site shutting down and the stock being on the verge of getting dropped by the NASDAQ since it went under a dollar, and Barry asked him about the chances that investors would come in now that things were at their worst, something he called the "Dead Cat Bounce," but Avery said he had no answers. The *Times* article, of course, referred to their own story, "The $3,000 Date." They said that Thad claimed to have introduced the apple martini to New York.

Avery held my hand as we climbed up to my garret.

He told me he had indeed been in a panic, the Monday after our night together in August. The Friday before, the investment bankers sold some stock for Avery and Thad, as had been planned. A lot of what Avery realized went to pay off the credit cards he'd been living on for months, from before the time of the IPO. But then, that Sunday, he learned Thad had gone off and cashed more, and Thad made it clear he wanted to grab what he could and let the business fall. They'd had a huge fight. He'd been about to tell me, but when I was so remote, he figured I was one of those women who don't want any strings attached to sex.

"I was trying to be cool," I said.

"Cool?" he said. "Cold as Kelvin."

"Who's Kelvin?"

"Kelvin's the scale that starts at absolute zero. That's what you were, minus 459."

"Only a nerd knows that," I said, fondly.

Then we lurched together.

Steam

Avery's living here, down a theoretical 6 million. He clears a bit on the apartment sublet. Real estate continues strong: eBrightlights' most valuable asset turns out to be the lease on the office. Avery has to go into the city from time to time, because of the bankruptcy proceedings, but mostly he hangs around our house. He starts books but doesn't finish them. He paid for us to get a DSL connection and set up his computer on Granny Lou's desk. Barry's thrilled to be able to bid on eBay with split-second timing.

In fact, my brother is altogether enthralled with Avery, who he respects as a man with vision, sure to bounce back. He's convinced items from the early days of eBrightlights.com will be collectibles, relics of the dot.com boom and bust. He got Avery to sign sheets of eBrightlights stationery (part of my haul) which he taped to the bottom of each salvaged chair along with copies of the relevant articles, establishing provenance. Last week Barry took Avery over to Queens to pick up a never-opened case of 1960s Aqua Velva, and on the way back over the Verrazano Bridge, where the proximity of New York and New Jersey is so clear, showed him the layout of the harbors and airports, the essential unity of the region, and offered Avery his theory about racism as a form of waste and all the money to be made investing in Newark, trying to get him interested in New Jersey real estate. Barry's counting on something being left when they settle with creditors, to fund a new venture. Avery speaks of freelancing, building web pages, working from home. But then late at night he tells me that every new technology had its bust before it took hold—did I know Fulton went broke on steam and came back? Who knows what the future holds, but for now, we're together.

Meanwhile, the coverage goes on. In February the *Wall Street Journal*, which is so hypocritical if you ask me, all those guys sitting on what they raked in because of those poor entrepreneurs at whom they're scoffing now, ran a piece on the extravagance of the boom times, citing the eBrightlights chairs. It mentioned, in passing, as if it were more evidence of Thad and Avery's over-ambition, that they'd hired me, "a top-tier literary editor," quoting the great Peter Alphonse Delisle (reached in retirement in Montclair) saying, inaccurately, that I'd been groomed as his heir—and next thing you know, I got this call from a software tycoon turned philanthropist who bought The Stylus name and logo and subscriber list, asking me to edit the revived magazine.

Yes, we have a website, but you have to pay to get your hands on our full content. In print. Bi-monthly. We're a glossy— thin, slick paper with photos. With the blessing of my backer, I'm jazzing up the Poe connection, with an article tracking the Dead Woman Fetish through the past hundred and sixty years, from Pre-Raphaelite beauties to today's Goth girls, in the launch issue, May/June, just out. There's a regular column on the money chase called The Gold Bug. At my insistence, we're listing Peter Alphonse Delisle, who will be contributing reminiscences from *The Stylus* of yore, as Editor Emeritus—in fact, on the masthead, we're listing all of the editors for the past 102 years, from Richard Pentreath Hodges and Edward Lydon Clare down to me, Mary Louise Sottile. I've hired a bright young graphic designer, some grateful out-of-work writers, and, yes, as Ad Director, my friend since high school, Celie, who was on the verge of moving in with her parents. She says, privately, that *The Stylus* will always lose money for its owner, but he knows what's best for his tax return, and I think we may catch on. According to the piece on us in the *Times*, well, according to me in the piece, people are yearning for ancestry, for continuity, for all the twists of a tale.

Not that I believe the Web is dead. Thank you for checking out my personal site, AttentionSurplus.com. Please enter your e-mail address below to receive future offers.

One Hippopotamus

Lightning: I wake to the flash, see Carlos's clothes, the surface of a man thrown over the chair. He vanishes. I keep my eyes open, trying to make out his real body beside me in the dark, and wait for the thunder. Earlier, in the restaurant, we saw the forecast, lines of storms across the state. The Fort Lauderdale station lavishes technology on its star meteorologist. He has a computerized map table where with a touch he can go close, showing neighborhoods as the radar crosses them, green with orange centers of rain. With each sweep the display jumps, tracking the storm cells' advances, how far they travel in a minute. On the edge of dream I picture us as the radar sweeps by, showing our cool blue shoulders and hot crotches, unmistakably new lovers.

The thunder unfolds, still miles west.

Carlos turns away, into the pillow, and groans.

I prop myself up. The room is resolving into shapes and layers. I look appreciatively at his leg's dark curve on top of the sheet. I'm trying to make sure I enjoy this, the good part. Too often I have peeked ahead and seen this one isn't going to last, like ruining a book by reading the final page. He's thirty-seven and never married, there's undoubtedly something wrong with him, but why do I need to know that now? Anyway, there's something wrong with all of us.

Light licks the mirror.

"One Mississippi," whispers Carlos. "Two Mississippi—"

"Where'd you get that?"

"—sippi. Four—I'm counting seconds. Ah," he says to the thunder, "there we go. Five miles away."

"I know. I mean, where did you learn to count by Mississippis? You didn't say that in Chile, did you?"

"No. I was so young when I left I don't remember how we measured thunder."

"In my family, we counted hippos. One hippopotamus, I think it's a little slower than Mississippis. Hippopotamus. Mississippi. See? How much is a second?"

A double flash reveals the bedroom, bathroom, and the closet beyond that's my workspace. "We're in for it," he says. "Want something to drink?"

"Sure. Anything." I resist the impulse to offer to get up and get it myself. It's my tiny cottage. But I'm going to let him think I'm someone who gets treated well. He comes back with the bottle of pinot grigio we started earlier, juice glasses. He pours for us with a flourish and gets in beside me, everything about him signaling: Nice guy.

Carlos runs a remodeling business, specializing in Deco restorations. That's how I met him; he hired me to do the graphics for a brochure showing their work and he persuaded me to tour some projects, see how well he knew what the clients moving in from up north wanted, how he knew architectural history as well as light fixtures. He's almost ostentatiously an American guy. Many people call him Charlie. He's baseball-loving, wears nice polo shirts and athletic shoes, has a good haircut but not too good. His father was among the disappeared in Chile and his mother sent Carlos to his aunt in Florida, to protect him. Once he was gone she made noise, seeking his father, and then she died ambiguously, a car hit her, no way to know from afar what happened. He was left, an orphan with his aunt, in America. Of course, I love this story. I suspect many women have.

We kiss a little. I'm sore, from earlier, though willing, but he just pats me, as if to say, hello, I know you're there. He sits up with his hands behind his head, listening. The thunder crawls over us. "You have a good surge suppressor, right?"

"Not one I trust. I unplugged the computer, before we went out to dinner. My power goes out all the time."

"Florida gets the most lightning strikes of any state," Carlos says. "Did you know that?"

"I know golfers are always getting zapped. The state is all water."

"Yeah, water and limestone," he says. "Porous."

I picture the peninsula, sprawled out like me, full of holes, defenseless.

We're in light so bright I can see the whole of this room and the next, as if they were x-rayed. The thunder follows fast, and the storm casts the first big drops, hard as pebbles, against the roof. "You're right," he says, "hippopotamus takes longer."

Something charged smacks down and he says, "That was a big one," just as there's a loud pop outside and the power goes off.

The dark is deeper—no LED display from the clock radio. The answering machine light is out. After a minute, the ceiling fan drifts to a halt and there's no air at all. The air conditioning is gone—a kind of death, the cessation of the house's usual cool damp wheezing. The rain roars. Florida rain—there should be a special word for it. There's no separation of drops. Not sheets of rain. Blocks of it.

"I'm going to get you a good surge suppressor," he says.

"Hmm," I say, "are you sure you want to suppress my surges?"

"Not all of them."

The electric show goes on above us. "Rock and roll," he says, and reaches down to pour himself more wine. I finish mine to catch up.

"Marianne," he says.

"I'm Jenny."

"No, no, no, I know that. God. Marianne is the one who taught me to count Mississippis."

"Who was she?"

"She was my girlfriend. In college."

"A Southerner I guess. If she counted Mississippis."

"Sure," he says. "You know I went to college in Gainesville.

That's part of the South."

I don't want to ask. What does it matter where he's been before? But I know I must. It's time for this part. "So," I say, "what happened?"

"We drank a lot. Marianne liked liqueurs in layers, stuff with silly names. Woowoos—I forget what was in those. We'd drink till we got sick."

"Do drugs?"

"When we could get them. I didn't have much money. And I worked too hard for it. Never been very druggy. Boring. Sorry." He gives me the nice guy smile. "Anyway, we really didn't have that much to say to each other when we weren't drunk, but for some reason I didn't pay attention to that."

"Was she gorgeous?"

"You're just trying to make trouble here."

"You can tell me," I say.

"I'm not that dumb. She had blond hair, in that style with the bangs going back like wings girls had then. It looks funny now, but at the time it was very sexy."

"That style was already out then."

"Not in the South," he says.

"Okay, she was gorgeous," I say. "Enough about that."

"She was planning to be a lawyer and she liked to argue. Much more than I did. She came from a small town in orange country. Her parents came and took us out to dinner, the first time they met me, in the spring. I put on a suit and tie. The suit was so ugly, a pale blue, with this fake scratchy texture. I'd gotten it for high school graduation and then I'd grown another inch. So it was too small, also. I'm sure I looked ridiculous. And I expected her father to hate me. I mean, you're a guy who's sleeping with his daughter and you're sure he can tell. It's normal."

The rain has eased. I can hear the gush of water from the overflowing gutters, going down along the bathroom wall where the plaster has been repaired before.

"I didn't expect to hate him. I'd worked as a waiter, down here, in the summer, at a fancy place, and we'd see men like him. Some people react very strangely to being the customer, it seems to fill them with rage. He was one of those. The mother was—you know—apologetic. And Marianne had a way of making fun of his demands, saying the truth, 'Oh Daddy don't be a jerk,' lightly, which didn't seem to bother him. But I was just paralyzed with hatred. I could hardly speak. It wasn't just what he was doing, running the waitress around, sending food back, insisting he'd ordered something he hadn't, speaking in this condescending way, refusing to look at her. I'd seen all that before, and I imagined the waitress was getting even some way—you know, put some eye drops in his drinks to give him the runs, spit on his food, stuff like that. I just somehow knew that this man, if he'd been in a place like Chile, he'd be one of the ones who hurt people. And I was one of the ones he'd like to hurt." He laughs softly. "It's crazy, right?"

"I don't know. I guess I'd have to see him."

"I've never been political. I never wanted to be, you know, caught with the obsession, stuck in the past. This wasn't really political though. It was just instinctive. Maybe hormonal. Maybe we were just like two dogs over her. Maybe that's what politics really are, you know. We didn't really say anything. But I knew he was planning to get her away from me.

"When summer came she got an internship with a law firm, up in D.C. Her father lined it up for her. He paid her way and bought her a brand-new convertible. I worked at the restaurant in Miami Beach and took a summer course down here. When we spoke on the phone, after 'I miss you' there wasn't much else to say, nothing of substance. The relationship would have faded off, but I didn't want him to beat me. So I told her how in love I was and how hot I was over the phone and made her, you know, say the same. I was being the fascist too, wanting to control.

"Her internship was ten weeks and then she went home. I borrowed a friend's car and drove up there. The town was as she had described it, white houses with porches, moss on the trees. Very hot. I got a motel room at the edge of the next town, then drove by their house. Her car was out front, with the top up, but the windows were partly open. In that kind of town, no one dreams of crime. Their house was maybe not as big as I'd imagined. In my mind he was rich. I could have gone up and knocked on their door, but no, no, I didn't trust them. I parked a block away, and wrote a note for her, and then I casually walked past and dropped it into her car, on the front seat. I asked her to meet me at my motel and run away with me and get married."

"Wow," I say.

"Yes," he says. "Romantic, right? The motel was one of those places with maybe ten units, a row of boxes, pretty old. Every room had a metal chair out front. The ice machine was broken. I remember I was in agony about whether I could leave for a few minutes to get ice. I left her a note, but of course when I got back she hadn't showed. I had ice and a six-pack and some pretzels, and settled down to wait. It was a long night. There were thunderstorms, like tonight, big ones. Lots of wind knocking branches off the pine trees behind the motel. I was imagining that they'd locked her in or something. Or maybe she wouldn't even see the note till morning.

"And then she showed up." Carlos laughs. "Drunk as shit. Fell right over the metal chair on the way in. She'd gotten my note when she went out with her friends. Spent the evening drinking at a party and working up her nerve. She'd gotten into the spirit, though, the whole sneaky thing. She went home and pretended to go to bed and then loaded up a suitcase and tiptoed out to me. Can't imagine how they didn't hear her, because at my motel she was crashing around. Full of peppermint schnapps. She'd had her hair cut up north—shorter, curly. She looked good, it wasn't that, but she kissed me and I knew I didn't love her. Simply that, I didn't. For the first time in months, I started thinking.

"What was I doing? I was twenty years old. I didn't even have enough money to own a car. I didn't want to marry some girl and wreck my life. Hers too. So maybe her father would have been a fascist if he had the chance. But he didn't. He couldn't do a thing to me except maybe keep me out of his country club. This thought had been sneaking up on me all summer, but for some reason I couldn't really see it till then. That's how it is. Things change in a second and then you understand how it was coming all along."

"So did you tell her the elopement was off?"

"I didn't know how to do that. All I could think to do was delay. So I told her we were too drunk to drive right then, and the weather too bad, and took her to bed."

"Oh, that was mean."

"Bad thing to do, huh? Making love on false pretenses. But actually we'd barely begun when she got up and was barfing in the bathroom. Truly a romantic evening. She took a shower, then complained because those towels were so thin. She came back to bed—still drunk. She had the whirlies, so we didn't start up again. I remember her counting the seconds as Mississippis, to figure out how near the storm was, and when we could leave. She was all lovey-dovey. I held her and got her to go to sleep, promising I'd wake her when we could go. And then I lay there thinking how I could get out of it. I tried to think of some way to get her to reject me."

"Why couldn't you just tell her you'd thought better of it?"

"That seems simple now, I know. But then—I'd never been honest with a girl. I didn't even know you were supposed to be. I kept thinking I wasn't supposed to hurt her. Or get her mad. Among guys, you know, lore gets passed around, how women go ape when they're rejected. Most of it wrong, no doubt, but when you're a young guy, you're trying to find out about women."

"But you don't ask the women."

"Oh no. That would never do. You are absolutely terrified that they'll find out you don't already know it all. Are you kidding?"

I snort.

"Ah," he says. "Mad at me?" He puts an arm around me.

We're silent in the room. It's mildly suffocating. Thunder crawls over us again. We are inside the belly of a giant.

He gets up and goes to the bathroom. While he's in there, I light a vanilla candle and pick my shirt off the floor and put it on. I don't want to be naked and thinking of the ways men have found to dump me, their evasions, their transparent lies.

He comes back and smoothes the sheets before he sits.

"How'd you get rid of her?"

"I don't think I'll tell you."

"Okay," I say. "Don't." I think how late it is, how burned out I'll be tomorrow. I could just go to sleep, but I know he's going to tell me.

"Just remember, I was young." He sighs. "I sat there for hours, making up ridiculous excuses: I really loved someone else or I had made a vow of some kind or I had a secret illness, all the while listening to the air conditioner in the wall grind away. I thought about how my mother must have loved my father, what amount of love was really necessary for marriage, and I was ashamed to have trivialized it. And then, I realized I was listening hard, waiting for the noise that would be her father. I saw that was my only hope, that he would arrive. My rescuer. I prayed for him to notice she wasn't home. What would he do? Call the police? They'd find her car. Perhaps they'd come get her. But somehow I thought he'd show up himself. I got dressed, I remember, to wait for him. Before dawn I heard a truck start up and leave. I was afraid she'd wake up soon. I don't know why it seemed that if we left there we'd certainly get married, but it did. And so I went out to the pay phone and called him."

"You did? Really? And what did you say? I've got your daughter here?"

"No, I was a complete coward. He picked up the phone, and I whispered, as if I were someone else giving him a tip. I imagined he'd think I was some local, maybe the motel clerk. 'Your daughter's at the Owl Motel with some guy, room number 6.' He didn't say anything, and I thought, what if he's used to this, her winding up drunk in motels. So I added, 'They're running away together.' I hung up. I stood out there for a while, looking at the light change, the dripping trees and spooky vapor rising from the ground. I remember thinking this is the worst thing I've ever done. Then I went back to our room that stank of peppermint and barf and woke her up and told her to get dressed, it was time to go. I didn't want him to find her in the bed. While she was in the bathroom I heard a car pull up, right outside, beside hers. He knocked. I opened the door for him, and I called to her that he was there."

"Did he charge in?"

"He wasn't in a rage, you know. He looked quite scared. Or, now I think of it, hung-over. A red-faced man with shaking hands. When she came out of the bathroom he said, 'Marianne, you've got to come home,' not loud or anything.

"She said, 'Daddy, we're getting married.'

"'No, you couldn't be,' he said, and he looked at me. I was sitting on the bed, being as quiet as I could, filled, really, with relief.

"While she put on her shoes and started throwing things into her suitcase, he was going on, about how low I was to have her sneaking away instead of offering to marry her properly, which was of course very true. I couldn't contradict it. I sat there with my head down.

"And he said, 'I told you, the first time I met him. He's not like us.' She said, 'Oh, Daddy,' and he said, 'Not even the same species.'"

I reach and touch his arm. "That's horrible."

"That's what he said. And, you know, the thing is, she smiled. She smiled. I think she liked him saying that. She picked me out because I was what would bother her daddy the most. That must have added to her thrill, all along. Mating with another species."

I can think of nothing to say to this. I just rub my hand on his arm. "So what happened then?"

"She snapped her suitcase shut and came over to me and said, 'Are you ready? Can we leave now?'

"And so I didn't get out of it at all. I had to say, 'Marianne, you should go home. We'd never make it together.' And maybe she could tell everything that was wrong with me. Because she didn't argue, which was odd, for her. She grabbed her suitcase. At the door, she said, 'I expected you to be brave.'"

I laugh. "Dramatic. But you can't blame her."

"Of course. Then she drove off in her convertible, with him following, on guard. And I got up and drove back to Miami in my buddy's car, dizzy and playing loud music to stay awake."

"What happened to her?"

"I don't know. I did hear she went to law school. I assume she's rich and married and all that."

"Or in therapy, or all messed up. I feel sorry for her."

"Jenny, I bet you always feel sorry for the girl." He puts his hand on my knee.

"Yes, I suppose so. You've got me there. I've been the girl, you know, can't help it." I yawn. Our smells rise around us, the vanilla candle no disguise. I wonder if I should send him home. I feel the temptation to have my solitude and rest, but still I like this, having him telling me stories in the dark. "You never talked to her?"

"I saw her from afar that next year at school, but never since then."

"And how did you feel when you saw her?"

"Embarrassed, but I have to admit, Jen, mostly I was happy to be free. The whole thing had given me the idea that love was nothing but possessiveness and turmoil. I told myself I'd learned."

"What?"

"Well, I'm afraid the first thing I learned was to make sure from the start of dating someone that I had an out."

"Oh, nice. So many men do that. What was yours?"

"Well, for a while I told girls that I was carrying the torch for Marianne."

I groan.

"It wasn't entirely untrue. I was getting over her, wasn't I? Sometimes I missed her. But eventually," he says, "I outgrew excuses and learned not to say more than I meant. That was the real problem, after all."

"Was it?"

"Partly. I also realized I had to wait for someone of my own species, whatever that might mean." He is looking at me hard in the candlelight.

I feel how tired I am, the room floating oddly. I wonder why he told me this story. Is this all a roundabout way of breaking up?

"Jenny." He rolls toward me and loops his leg over mine. "My God, you're sweet," he says.

"Do you like me, then?"

He demonstrates his liking. After a while, I pull off my shirt. He's above me, a warm shape in the dark.

"What do you say, Jenny," he asks, "might we be the same species?"

I hold my breath and feel the whole weight of him, his sad Chilean orphaning, the neatness with which he arranges his possessions, strong hands, furious driving, nice guy smile, passionate allegiance to the Baltimore Orioles, detailed knowledge of space-age countertop materials, cowardice in a crisis, honesty—anything might be a rift someday, but for some reason I have a crazy shred of hope I've never felt before. I breathe, "We might be."

"I'm serious," he says. "Are you serious?"

The answering machine beeps, back on the job. We laugh and go on. The ceiling fan shudders and picks up speed. When we're done we spread out, letting it cool us. The clock has reverted to midnight, blinking. The rain is just a patter. And then lightning to the west again takes our picture.

"One hippopotamus," says Carlos.

Oh no, I think. I'm going to love him. I'll never get rid of him now.

Gossip and Toad

Tally McTeer left the Bubble Room and headed homeward, thinking through the last tidbits she'd call in for her column. After a week of rain, a fine evening brought out crowds on Lincoln Road. Twin Apollos rollerbladed by, the mistress of a deposed dictator pushed a corgi in a baby carriage, and women who were women jostled women who were not—but these were merely people who wanted to be seen. Tally was on the lookout for the hidden, the half-hinted, some slip.

From a table outside Fungi, Vic Fenton, a music publicist, hailed her. He introduced his party: Rozalee, "the fantastic new young singer-songwriter," the producer Graff Bryant, and a couple of business types connected to Rozalee's debut album, all in town for the video awards this weekend. Fenton wanted a picture taken, and, since he gave her items sometimes, Tally phoned and caught her photographer heading back to the office.

Tally took a seat across from Graff Bryant. She waved off a drink and studied Bryant's long, serious face. He'd been a singer-songwriter, too, before he moved on to work with others. Rozalee was a pretty girl, exotic. What had Tally heard of her? Father

Brazilian, mother American, or the other way around? She looked sensuous but oversensitive, like someone easily crushed.

Or perhaps Rozalee was just feeling crushed right now. Tally noticed the way Graff's shoulder overlapped hers. Was he touching her? Protective or . . . something else? Tally ignored their faces, which were attentive to the conversation, and watched their bodies. Graff's arm stretched along the back of Rozalee's chair, the sleeve of his shirt rolled up enough to show a strong forearm. How old was he now, 34, 35? And this Rozalee looked 20.

No big deal. Often the producer and the produced hooked up. But they were being covert, Tally felt. Still in the new stage, or maybe no one had yet made a definitive overture. A tiny pulse moved in Rozalee's throat, just above her collarbone. Her head leaned back. Yes, her dark hair was brushing Graff's shirt.

The photographer arrived and Tally stood to give her a clear angle for pictures. "Ilana will double-check the captions," Tally said, and she excused herself and left. She reached the end of Lincoln, walked a block up Alton Road, and then crossed the little bridge to where her condo tower rose beside the Intracoastal.

She took her laptop and the one drink she allowed herself each night, a small fino sherry, out onto her balcony. She loved this location. From the eighth floor she could see the lights of traffic on the beach, and along the Intracoastal the slow, expensive progress of yachts. Others wanted to gaze out at the ocean, but she liked to see humans in action. The ocean was, though of course one couldn't say this, so boringly natural. In Florida it wasn't that easy to get away from nature. This humid September night was full of buzzes and croaks from unseen creatures.

The last photos came through on her e-mail. Tally's assistant Alden, looking at them too, phoned. He was still at the office, at the other end of Lincoln, near the oceanfront hotels where so many of their subjects stayed. She could hear the squawks of his police radio in the background. He'd keep it on into the wee hours, in case there was some interesting trouble.

"We'll use one of Little Nita at the Bubble Club, of course," he said.

Little Nita, hot for the past three years, was often in the column. Her face at 18 was masklike above her chainmail halter. "She'd better watch out," Tally said. "She looks so dissatisfied and hard."

"The baby fat is going," said Alden.

"Yes," Tally said. "To be a smutty baby is cute, but to be a smutty woman is not." She coughed. She had a bug in her mouth. Something had flown in, a gnat or no-see-um. "Phth." She picked it out and looked at the screen.

"Who's this?" said Alden. "With Rozalee."

"Oh, Graff Bryant." Ilana had caught some sadness in his long face. "He's looking not so fabulous," said Tally. "As if he'd actually had a thought in his life. Why's he here?"

"He produced that song of Rozalee's in the video," Alden said. "Haven't you seen it?"

"Not yet, I guess."

"Well, it's great. Rozalee's gay, you know."

"Aren't they all?" said Tally. She's gay, he's gay, that's what Alden said of everyone. He insisted that there'd been at least five gay presidents so far, including Lincoln. Alden was, of course, gay.

"No," Alden said, "I mean, she's openly gay, that's part of her thing, that she's sincere and young and gay. She has this video where she and her lover, this muscly fighter girl, are being hounded by the homophobes and she's singing about secret love but it's no secret, you see?"

"Well, Alden, I could absolutely swear to you that she's having a thing with Graff Bryant," said Tally.

"No!" he said.

"Ah," she said. "Yes. That's the new shocker. Not homophobes, but faux homos."

Alden giggled. And so she tossed it into her column—the item, the quip, with question marks and nudges, not outright *saying* it of course, but still. Alden picked a photo where Rozalee and Graff were looking very close indeed. Tally watched the gossip shows she'd TiVoed and, after *Night Talk* with Jacqui Carter, went to bed.

***

But that night she felt ill and restless. She dreamed she had one earring and the other was lost in a roomful of earrings, thousands of them, and her task was to find the mate. She woke up tired and went to her desk. In this direction she could see the top of the Van Dyke Hotel, and, beyond it, the Delano's glamorous white Deco spire.

Alden had secured her admission to tonight's awards eve bashes, see-and-be-seen events, each a kind of mock party, where the celebs would be surrounded by security as they lounged and chatted in supposed carefree intimacy. Tally planned her progress, trying to figure out where the evening would crescendo.

The cell phone rang—Alden, calling early. He had a source at the Delano who said that Little Nita got pretty hammered last night. She was leaning on her bodyguard as she came into the hotel at 3 a.m.

"Well," Tally said, "backtrack it. Where was she?"

"I'll find out."

"She's ready to fall," said Tally. "Within five years she'll be playing lounges if she's lucky." And when she spoke, out of her mouth came three tiny lizards. "My God."

"What?" asked Alden, lazily curious.

"No, nothing—spilled something." The lizards had scooted off. She imagined they'd somehow crept into her mouth in the night—horrid as that thought was—and jumped out now. Geckos abounded here and sometimes she found one, emaciated and dried up, even on the 8th floor. Thank God she'd been on the phone, and no one could see her. She felt queasy but managed to sound stern, "Anything else?"

"No. It's always like this," Alden said. "No sooner does the column come out than we have to start all over filling it, and it inevitably takes us till the deadline."

"Well, something will happen: a nice murder or a politician's folly. I hear the mayor broke up with his blonde, so he'll be after a new one," she said, and a toad, a fat, little green toad, hopped from her mouth and sat on her wide pale desk, blinking his orange eyes. She gasped and coughed, and out poured spiders and millipedes. They skittered across the desktop and over its edge. The toad gave her a look and hopped after them.

"Have to go," she said, in a fit of coughing and disgust.

"Sounds like you're getting a cold," said Alden. "Take care."

She went to the bathroom and opened her mouth over the toilet, but nothing more came out, just a string of spittle. She looked through the medicine cabinet. Not much there beyond cosmetics. She had perfect health. Till now. She chewed an antacid, chalky, but she got it down. Then she gargled, spat, waited. Nothing. Still, she felt ill, very ill. Her body trembled.

Could she speak to a doctor? But a doctor might tell. She knew, none better, how ready people were to pass news along. Who could she confide in? No one.

She took a deep calming breath and decided to go to the gym. Exercise always made her feel better. She dressed and went out, avoiding her desk, hoping the creatures would just vanish. She walked down Alton quickly, erect, holding her mouth carefully shut.

***

Normally she loved coming here. The gym teemed with stories. Trainers often sold her little items. But today she kept to herself. She lay back on the abs machine and worked, thinking if she strengthened her core, it might help. What had caused this, what brought it on? But she knew, she knew—it was her work. It was as they always said, you could go on for years abusing yourself with no harm showing, but it's there all along, the slow peninsula of cholesterol in the arteries, the cells transmogrifying into some strange growth. Her problem was the poisoned words. But what could she do?

Gossip was in her blood. She'd grown up in Alabama, in a town where, among the many skilled practitioners of chat, the champion was her grandmother, a fat old lady who sat on her porch all day and served strong sweet tea to whoever came by and brought her some morsel of news. I've got the sugar, she would say, and indeed she did, if that meant diabetes, but it also described the way she would deplore a development while gloating, "Oh, isn't that a shame that he left her?" and "What a pity their youngest boy went bad." She knew, she sang the lines of descent and mismarriages of anyone mentioned. And little Tally listened, drinking from a thick glass jar, the tea's intensity only making her thirsty for more, till the smell of her dress, of her skin, was perfumed tannin, on that porch shaded with twining vines and honeysuckle's tiny trumpets. She had concealed this place of origin—tidied it out of her bio—but it was here she'd learned to gather shreds and twigs of information from which she could shape something.

She started her career in PR but couldn't manage the exuberant sell of the publicists, their fabulouses and fantastics. No, she was just too nasty and truthful. She crossed the line to professional gossip and began to build her following. Her little world buzzed with talk and speculation, her sources went out and brought word back to her, and bit by bit she increased her column's syndication. So far when she'd had chances to be on TV, she'd been too nervous and hard-edged, but she'd get there with work. And yet, here she was, ill from it. Yes, ill. She remembered last night, the gnat that had flown into her mouth. Perhaps it hadn't, perhaps it came *from* her—maybe it was the start. Or had there been other, earlier signs she'd somehow missed?

This might be like a dog having worms, she thought. Could she call a vet, describe her nonexistent pet, and get something that would scour out her insides? That seemed drastic, but when she thought of the bugs, the lizards, and especially that toad, she shuddered.

She went into the locker room, took another antacid, and belched faintly. She felt dizzy. What if she just ate something hearty? She was not like her grandmother, no, she was a size 4 and rationed herself: sushi, water, lettuce, soy. But maybe she'd dieted away her strength to resist whatever this was.

So off she went to lunch on Lincoln Road. At her regular cafe, where she was known for drinking her espresso at noon under the blue umbrella of their best people-watching table, they were surprised when she ordered actual food, but she felt some chicken salad and a roll couldn't hurt. And she was careful to say only the kindest things about the service.

Her paper, the fattest of the Friday tabs, had come out, freshly distributed this morning. She grabbed a copy and turned to her column: Tally's Rant. Here, her home base, they carried it all, words and pictures, but other cities that picked it up might take only part, use one photo or none. She looked at her own little headshot, her cool square glasses, her angled jaw. She already looked older than that. Others around her were reading the column. She could follow and tell when they hit—near the end—the innuendo that Rozalee was straight. It made them laugh. Knowing, heedless laughs: they all had a taste for that tiny bit of mean.

She ate a bite of chicken and gazed at a transvestite fabulosa passing by, showing how grandly louche to be. And then there was, oh my God, Rozalee herself, stalking down the block, heading right for her. She was lithe in a sports bra and what looked like a man's striped shirt artfully wrapped and tied around her waist, a Brooks Brothers sarong.

She stopped in front of Tally and waved the paper in her face. "What is this?" she said.

"Oh, honey, did it upset you?" This was wonderful. There was nothing better than provoking a reaction. The girl was young, or she'd know better.

"You have no idea what my life is," said Rozalee. Rio and New York mingled in her voice.

"Well, if I got it wrong, please tell me. Sit down, do." People were looking. Not that she minded. But Rozalee did sit, crossing her legs. Her flat sandals, Tally decided, were definitely gay.

"Anyone can be straight. Or gay. Or bi. It doesn't matter to me," Tally said. "I just heard something and passed it along. Is it a lie?"

"What's personal is personal," Rozalee said.

"Not when you make a video about it. That makes it a public issue, doesn't it?"

"If I write a love song, it doesn't matter who I wrote it for. If the feeling is there, anyone can imagine it is about who they themselves love. Perhaps you don't know enough about love to understand this?"

"That's very interesting," Tally said. "May I quote you?"

Rozalee shrugged and frowned, biting her lip. She was, Tally knew, trying to remember precisely what she'd said.

"Let me ask you something," said Tally. "I notice you haven't denied it. Are you involved with Graff Bryant?" She held out the tab, pointing to the picture of the two of them, Bryant's arm extended around Rozalee.

Rozalee stood up. "What is the point of you?"

"Is that," Tally said, waving at Rozalee's wrapped hips, "by any chance the shirt he was wearing, last night? Because—" She tapped the page. "I think I recognize it here. See?"

Rozalee looked stricken. "Leave him alone," she said. "No further comment."

Tally proffered a card. "Please call me anytime you'd like to talk. I'd be delighted to set the record straight." Though she tried, she could not keep from lingering on that last word. She felt her gorge rise and got her napkin to her mouth in time to spit into it a small cascade of grasshoppers, green as asparagus. When she lifted her head, Rozalee had stalked half a block off, bystanders looking after her swaying butt. A cute, angry girl, not too famous yet to walk alone on Lincoln Road.

Tally crushed the napkinful of bugs into her little straw purse. Her appetite was gone.

Normally she would have checked in at the office, but this would be a late night and she really didn't feel well. When she got home she forced herself to look around her desk, but saw no evidence of the creatures.

Relieved, she went in to run a bath, and found the toad sitting near the drain of her lovely tub with the high curved spigot. He seemed bigger and she thought perhaps he had eaten the others, the lizardy things, the bugs. He looked at her, those orange eyes trying to communicate—what?

"Can you speak?" she asked.

He said nothing.

"If I kiss you, will you turn into someone?"

He said nothing. He looked a little parched, she thought, his skin more yellow and bumpy than earlier. She turned the cool water on, just at a drip. He seemed to like that. He splashed a bit, but still he looked at her. "Were you too dry?" she asked.

Did she detect a bit of orange gratitude in those eyes?

"Now," she said, "shoo, because I need to take a bath." He gazed at her, that's all. Well, what can you do, she thought. She plugged the drain and turned the water full on—but kept it tepid—and got in, her spare little body at one end, his swimming lazily at the other.

He had sprung from her, and in an odd way that made him more acceptable. The way people didn't find their own children disgusting, perhaps, something Tally had heard of but never quite understood before.

When she let the water out, she lifted him from the tub. She wasn't sure whether he could get up the slippery sides of it. His skin wasn't slimy at all, but soft from the water, like her own. His warts, too, were soft, and colorful, more like ornaments than flaws. They gazed at each other, and then, feeling slightly hypnotized, she lay down for a short nap.

When she woke, she felt much better, ready for work. The toad—-she looked around—was out on the balcony, squatting in the shade under her chaise lounge.

***

At the office, Alden was fielding calls. The entertainment gossip world was gathering in Miami. Tonight they'd cover the meet-and-greet parties for performers, tomorrow the video awards themselves. They were looking for any fresh angle, and it seemed that Tally had this Rozalee-Graff story before anyone else, so she was invited to go chat about it on the local shows, on cable, and, best of all, Jacqui Carter from *Night Talk* wanted her.

Here it was, her chance for the big leap. And now all she could picture was leaning in to confide and opening her mouth and some goddamn thing coming out of her. She shuddered. Still, there was nothing to do but prepare.

She read Alden's research on Rozalee: 23 years old. Previous liaison: a high school girlfriend, with whom she'd started a band. They'd been together for a couple of years, broken up a year ago, and Rozalee went solo, got signed to do this album. Alden had located a copy of the first video and Tally watched it. Rozalee looked a bit of a gypsy here, and she could sing, with touches of the '60s, but fresh, too. In the video, the two lovers were dancing inside their little house while a rube looked through one window, then another, in leering anger. The nasty good old boy—who played him? Whose job was it to look like a stupid thug? Maybe some fellow from a place like her hometown had had theatrical ambitions and left, she thought, and then been doomed by his looks to play forever the kind of people he'd fled. That would be an interesting story, sometime. At the bridge of the song, he managed to bust in and hurt the hard-body girl. Rozalee held her, singing, then faced the bad guy down with sheer lung-power and blazing eyes.

"She was just friends with the girl in the video," Alden said. "A young actress. *She's* gay."

Tally sent Alden out to talk to his hotel sources, while she went on the Internet to learn: A toad lives more on land, frogs more in water. Toads have less developed legs and dry, warty skin. *Sapo* is toad in Spanish. Hers matched the picture of the Southern Spadefoot Toad. They go to the water to mate and give birth. She thought of the toad in the tub with her and shivered, but in a not unpleasant way. This was how people screwed up, of course. They accepted their own actions, no matter how they'd look to others. The fascination of what one could watch oneself do, she'd heard many an addict speak about it, in comeback interviews.

But what choice did she have? Could she quit? If she cashed it all in was there enough to go back home and hole up? And could she stand it, living as a recluse? How could she of all people take a vow of silence?

No, she could not give up. She went home to change for the publicity events, her on-camera appearances. Her heart was in her throat. Or something was. She thought if she spoke only kind things she'd get through, but could she do that?

The toad was there, in the bedroom, on the bench at the foot of her bed. "Sapo," she called him. The name seemed right. She leaned over and kissed his head, dry and cool. Nothing happened, except, she felt, he seemed to vibrate.

"Sapo," she said, "what will I do?" He looked at her. She laid out her outfit for the evening, her cute shoes. She opened her purse to switch the contents over to her evening bag, and as she pulled out the crumpled napkin the grasshoppers fell to the floor. They were tangled together, but here and there a leg waved. Sapo hopped down and snapped them up.

"Oh, you were hungry," she said. They eat live things, she remembered.

Her phone trilled—Alden. He'd found where little Nita'd been, last night, at a biker bar out on the edge of the Everglades, brought there by the security guy, with whom, apparently, she had something going. Alden was there now, talking to the regulars. She'd been drunk and got up on the bar and danced and flashed her breasts. There was a cell phone video; he'd seen it and of course bought it. She congratulated him and told him to get back to the office as fast as he could.

She hung up in triumph. "Got the slut," she said, and as the creatures, slugs, arced toward the floor, the toad intercepted them and swallowed.

"Ah," Tally said, "I see, Sapo, darling." And she squatted beside him.

***

Almost a week later, they lounged upon her balcony, she and Sapo. Since he preferred the shade, she'd set up an umbrella to shelter the chaise, where he sat, rather grandly, his legs splayed. His eyes followed her, while she, at the table, worked the phone.

Tally was so busy now, ever since her interview with Jacqui Carter. Calm, purged, when she sat on the temporary fake living room set of *Night Talk*, she'd spoken with gentle authority. "Jacqui, what Rozalee said to me was, 'What's personal is personal.' I think those were her exact words to me at lunch. And, you know, that's right. People can't help who they love."

"So you don't think this will hurt her with her fans?" said Jacqui, her eyes soft and concerned under her razor straight bangs.

"Well, as Rozalee says, people can apply the love in a song to their own situations. I think she'll just have more fans now. She's sincere, and sincerity," Tally said, sincerely, "is so, so rare. She's a talent and I wish her well."

"Do you think then this relationship with Graff Bryant will last?"

"Oh, I hope so," said Tally, sweetly, with just a shade of doubt, and she smiled for all she was worth. She'd found, finally, her tone.

Then Jacqui Carter showed the video of Little Nita, which Tally had sold her as an exclusive. They'd blacked out Nita's breasts, which was unnecessary since the video had been captured on the phone of someone pretty drunk and it was hard to see detail, but of course it looked much more risqué this way. Tally and Jacqui chatted sympathetically about the high cost of early fame. Next morning Little Nita was off to rehab, and Tally was signed up for semi-regular appearances on *Night Talk*.

The media had swarmed for shots of Rozalee on the red carpet at the video awards, where she entered alone, looking ambiguously lovely. By Monday, Rozalee's former girlfriend and bandmate had been tracked down by *Access Hollywood*, and she handled her interview well, saying Rozalee had never lied to her. On Tuesday, Graff and Rozalee appeared on *Entertainment Tonight*, holding hands. Graff Bryant seemed like a happy man, for now. Rozalee was so pretty and her skin looked amazing. She had something Tally had seen before, a kind of mysterious glow that comes from being discussed. Tally revised her view of Rozalee. Rozalee might last.

After the *ET* piece, Vic Fenton, the promoter, sent Tally a Prada purse filled with leopard-spotted green orchids and a tiny note saying "Thanks." Tally wondered whether, from the very start, he'd counted on her noticing the affair, whether he'd told Rozalee where to find her at lunch. If so, what could she be but grateful?

She moved her laptop to the chaise and sat near Sapo while she typed up her column. Word from the family of Little Nita's bodyguard was that he expected to marry her, while her people denied that and, by the way, announced that when she got out of rehab she was officially to be called just Nita, because she was a grown woman. Delicious stuff. Tally tried out each item upon the toad and he snapped up the juiciest results, looking at her with perfect trust.

The Noir Boudoir

On a warm Tuesday morning in late October, the tail end of the hurricane season, I sit in my car outside the Delphi and pretend I'm on stakeout: a honed tedium. Eight years retired, but you never stop being a cop. I sip coffee and look at the grand old building, recently rehabbed. The pressure-cleaned Sphinxes at the entrance cast sharp Sphinxy shadows, and fresh green awnings ripple up the front in the eastern ocean light as they must have in the Delphi's heyday. I think of all the stories the place could tell.

At least it's survived. On the next block I can see signs for a new tower touting luxury living: Buy your piece of sky. The boom has reached this area north of downtown. Deco buildings less cared for than the Delphi get knocked down and replaced by glass towers that can't emulate their glamour.

I'm parked behind Alex Sterling's white SUV, which was here when I arrived. Alex is young, gay, smart, a North Carolina boy with excellent manners and a work ethic. In three years he has built up quite a business: Sterling Estate Clearance. Old people die alone here in Miami and their children, living far away, often estranged or resentful, take what they want, and then Alex appraises, bids for, and disposes of the rest. With his respectful tone, open face, and name that rings true, they trust him. As do I, as much as I trust anyone.

Right now, I know, he is inside going through the late Mrs. Dorsett's pockets. Alex deals in fine china and what we call "smalls": jewelry, silver, personal doodads that he sells at high-end shows around the Southeast. He tells me that he learned the hard way that people hide their smalls, so now he combs through a place before we see it. He's found mine-cut diamonds in a denture case and a Rolex under the insole of a running shoe. To the finder go the spoils.

Which might be the motto for our team. When Alex has identified what he'll take, he brings us in for our specialties and we give him a price for what we want.

Hank Kussrow & Son, Jeff, double-park beside me in their furniture truck. Jeff Kussrow is the one with the knowledge about furniture, his dad the muscle. Hank's up in his 70s but still a big guy with thick gray hair. I've seen many a sideboard go downstairs on his back. He had a moving business, but his son is more into refinishing than lugging, Hank says, and persuaded him that's where the money is. We get out and make conversation about the weather and what Alex has told us so far: the estate is small but choice.

I hear from a block away a chug and backfire. "The old guy," says Hank, with a grin.

The old guy's van comes into view with his little white dog barking out the passenger window. Others of us may be variously old, but none as decrepit as him. Alex calls him Cash, which may be his name or the way he operates. He helps Alex, and then at the end Alex lets him take all the dreck. He sells the least likely things, rusty tools, old pots and pans, broken cameras, at the flea market in Ft. Lauderdale. He leaves the van running; it can take him a good six or seven tries to restart it. In his faded tropical shirt and disreputable shorts, with his longish white hair under a baseball cap and feet sockless in sneakers, he walks over just as Guillermo Reyes pulls up in his peach-colored panel truck inscribed *The Gizmo Man.*

Guillermo fixes clocks and radios and toasters. His shop on the beach sells a lot of mid-century kitchen stuff, from jelly glasses to Streamline Moderne blenders. Guillermo is a year or two older than me, in good shape, small, bald, and dapper. "Nice place," he says, as he joins us.

"We did a pick-up here last month," says Hank.

I say, "I wasn't called for that one." Guillermo shakes his head—not him either.

"Mostly crap," says Jeff. "The family took everything. All that was left was the bedroom set."

"Alex said it was good to get us in with the building," says the old guy, his voice frayed and shy. "And look, already, they've called us for another."

Sharon Lawler parks across the street. She waves, but doesn't get out. Sharon, as we all know, runs hot and must blast her air conditioning. She drives a wagon like mine but with purple tinted windows to prevent fading of the vintage clothes she sells on eBay.

These are my fellow members of the species Magpie. We are small-time antique dealers, which is to say we are collectors who sell to support our habit. We glean old things and send some on their journey up in price, which lets us make a buck and keep the treasures we cannot bear to part with. We'd be mere hoarders if we didn't sell.

Me? I'm Ray Strout. Old, but not that old: 63, retired cop, good pension, bad arteries, but I keep going. I'm into paper ephemera. Books, magazines, letters, photos, bills, matchbooks, anything like that interests me. There's history in paper. The card for a boxing match, a punched train ticket, the menu of a dinner in honor of a later-indicted honcho—these fascinate me. I take apart vintage magazines for the ads, back them with cardboard, wrap them in plastic, and sell them on Lincoln Road on Sundays in the season. One *House Beautiful* from the '40s can yield two dozen sales at ten to fifteen bucks each.

Alex comes out and waves and hops in with the Kussrows, who drive around the left side of the building, past the bougainvillea-draped stucco wall that hides the service entrance. We parade behind. Back here the balconies look out on Biscayne Bay. I gaze up at the building: twelve stories of curves and niches to break up the wind and survive a hurricane. When the glass towers collapse, the Delphi will weather on.

The truck backs up against the loading dock, while the rest of us park nearby. I get out one of the old suitcases I use for hauling off my finds. My stuff, thank God, is light. The old guy's van expires in a series of snorts. He leaves the dog there with the windows rolled down. From the back he takes out the first of many much-used liquor store cartons in which he'll pack up smalls for Alex.

There's not enough room in the freight elevator for all of us at once, so Alex takes me, Guillermo, and Sharon up first. Guillermo has his satchel full of flannel sheets—he likes to swaddle his gizmos lovingly. Sharon—her hair tinted the color of cherry Coke and her chest draped with lots of amber beads—carries her capacious purse. Most clothes she'll take right on their hangers.

Alex sends the freight elevator back down, and we follow him along the 6th floor hallway which smells of last night's dinners to Mrs. Dorsett's place. Alex unlocks the door and we're in 6-D.

"Nice," says the Gizmo Man. He's looking at the Grundig Majestic stereo hi-fi/radio in its cabinet. But I echo, "Nice." The living room is '50s Louis Quinze with pale blue sofa and chairs grouped around a coffee table. Alex shows us an elaborate silver lighter/cigarette dispenser: you lift the top and cigarettes rise like petals of a flower. Alex has marked it and the crystal ashtray with his red stickies: he's into tobacciana. Sheers cover the French doors to the balcony so the bay is just a pale blue suggestion. There's a small kitchen to our left and, opening from it and the living room, a dining area where the hutch flutters with Alex's stickers. To the right there's a hall, down which Alex leads us. He opens the bedroom door with a flourish.

Light slants through actual Venetian blinds, striping the pure Deco circle of the mirrored dressing table. The slipper chair. The ivory satin padded curving headboard of the bed. Sherry breathes, "My God, the noir boudoir," and so it is.

"Great, isn't it?" says Alex.

The Kussrows come in behind him with the old guy peeking between their shoulders.

"A veritable time capsule," says Alex. "Listen, there's a lot in here for Sherry and Ray. You folks," he says to the Kussrows, "do the big pieces in the living room first. Cash, I need you to pack up all the stuff from the hutch, and then Hank and Jeff can get the dining room set. We'll get the furniture from in here last."

Sharon dives into the closet while I move around, scanning for what I'll take. Books fill the lower shelves of both bedside tables. In a nook there's a lady's bill-paying desk. I glance at a picture on top of it in an etched Lucite frame. Alex hasn't marked it, so maybe the frame doesn't interest him, but I'll have to check. Lucite has value these days. I can always use frames and I like the picture. I assume it's the dead lady in her youth: white skin, full lips, beautiful curve of nostril and brow, the eyes pale under carved eyelashes. She's a babe. Her hair lifts from a side part and cascades. She's vaguely familiar, like a minor movie star.

I get a queen-size sheet from the linen closet and spread it out to protect the bedspread; the satin looks glamorous with the matching pillowcases propped against the headboard. I open my suitcase on top of the sheet and lay the picture down next to it. I check the bedside table drawers. Spot a great little notepad holder, embossed leather. Mechanical pencil. Several matchboxes from restaurants. A double set of playing cards for bridge, shagreen boxed. I'm making a mental tally of what I'll offer Alex. I put things in my case but it stays open for his inspection. I toss a hankie over to the other side of the bed, for Sharon's pile.

Guillermo comes in to get the bedside clock radio: '60s tortoise plastic.

"Hubba hubba," he says, looking at the picture. "Nice frame, too."

Sharon comes out of the closet with an armful of suits and asks, "That her?" and looks and says "Oh." She lays the suits down on her side of the bed. "Alex," she calls, "what did you say her name was?"

"Dorsett," he says, coming in. "Helena Dorsett."

"The lovely Helena Dorsett," says Sharon. "What do you know. I didn't see an obit."

I ask, "Was she an actress?"

"Femme fatale," says Sharon, enjoying the effect. I notice that the others have come to the door to see what's going on.

"Well, tell us," Alex says.

"She was a singer, for a while, I believe," says Sharon, "but then she married. Twice. It was when the second husband got killed that she became notorious."

"Both husbands?" I ask.

Sharon nods. "I was in the ninth grade, so it was 1963. They lived in the Gables. They were society people. Dorsett—husband number two—was trampled to death by a horse he owned, in the stables at Hialeah. And then it came out that her first was run down when he was crossing Collins, a few years before."

"A theme," I say. "Death by transportation." They nod at me. They know I was a cop up north. Mine was a small dying New Jersey city, troubled, but not a patch on what Miami has to offer.

"Well, the first was just an accident, as far as I recall. But in the second husband's case they found he had been murdered. Not by her. She was nowhere near the stables."

"Stable boy?" says Guillermo. "Jockey?"

"Another horse owner?" I say.

"No," she says. "The vet."

"Aah," I say. "Did something to the horse?"

"It had to do with drugging the horse, yes. This was so long ago, I'm surprised I remember it at all. I know I read a lot of stories about her in the newspaper. They as good as implied that she caused it or it was done because of her."

"Was she tried?" I ask.

"No. But she was smeared in all the papers. You know how it is when there's a good-looking woman. It has to be her fault, right?"

Guillermo and I look at each other and laugh.

"You guys," Sharon says.

"What about the vet?" I say.

"That was one reason there was so much coverage of the trial—everyone was waiting for him to implicate her, but he maintained it was an accident. I remember lots of reporting about her crowd, her house in the Gables, and then they went back into her past, because I saw this same picture, and I think it's from when she was younger and singing."

"Well, folks," says Alex. "However much this adds to the price of anything, we still need to pack up." Which is his polite way of getting us to work. The others back out, and Guillermo takes the clock radio and goes.

I point at the picture. "You want it?" I ask Alex casually, meaning may I have it. I keep my tone cool, because if I express desire he'll think it's worth something and keep it.

Alex hesitates, but then says, "Hey, it's yours."

I wrap a towel from the linen closet around the picture and put it in my case.

Sharon says, "Her clothes, I'll tell you, are first rate. All these St. John suits cost something, and they're well-cared for." She drapes more on her side of the bed.

I cart my case over by the desk and seat myself to go through it. With her story in mind, I take a little extra care. She's kept things tidy, and, as Sharon says, she liked quality. The desktop blotter holder is pale blue leather and a matching stationery case holds Crane's paper for notes and thank-yous. In the top drawer I find various business cards, but no address book. I'm always careful not to take financial records the estate might need, but I don't see any. In a folder labeled "Auto" there are expired insurance cards for a series of midsize sedans, and a prior driver's license from the '80s, but not the current one, if she was still driving. Helena Dorsett, d.o.b. April 17, 1928. A handsome older lady with gray hair—you can see the bone structure from the early portrait—and then my mind makes a shift and I recognize her. "Hey," I say, surprised. "I met her."

"Where?" calls Sharon. I hear her opening dresser drawers, her beads clicking. Leaning back in the desk chair, I can see her bending over the bottom drawer. Her hair has fallen around her face and I try to picture what she looked like in ninth grade: a kid with a flip. In 1963 I was in the Navy and skinny as a rail.

"On Lincoln Road a few times on Sunday mornings. She'd be well dressed, as you say, in a suit. And pleasant. She bought some crossword puzzle books I had, and then she'd ask for them each time she saw me. Said she liked to do them before she went to sleep. A well-preserved old lady, I'd have said. A femme fatale? You never know."

"Look at this," Sharon says. "Longline elegance." She holds up a beige foundation garment—bra to girdle all in one.

I look away. This business is disgusting, sometimes. We settle back to work. Sharon takes a load down and returns, complaining about how hot it's getting, and Alex kicks up the air conditioning for her. I lug my first case down and bring back another. I poke my head in the kitchen where the old guy is wrapping the barware, and I ask him to save me any cookbooks. He points to a stack. I grab a *Joy of Cooking*, an *Esquire Book of Cocktails*, a few recipe brochures put out by companies. One, *Chafing Dish Cookery*, is '60s, I'd say, from the illustrations. People collect these, believe it or not.

The sofa is gone, and the Kussrows are carting out the dining room table, murmuring to each other as they always do, "Left, a little left. More. Now, right, now." Guillermo is taking albums out of the stereo cabinet and fitting them into vintage carrying cases he has for them. "Put some tunes on," I suggest. He pulls out a middle period Sinatra, and Frank fills the apartment with regret.

Alex sits on the remaining upholstered chair, boxing up ashtrays he's collected from around the apartment, most of them Wedgewood, and the cigarette lighter/dispenser. "Let me have a few smokes," I say, and he dumps them beside me. He likes tobacciana, not tobacco. I put them in a silver case I carry. This is a deterrent, not an affectation; it helps to have to open it and consciously take one out. I've got myself down to three cigarettes a day. I can maintain like that forever, but if I try to quit, I'll swing back with a binge. Better this way.

"There were no other pictures?" I say. Again, casually.

"There were some family photos, but the daughter took those. Not sure why she left that one."

"She had a daughter?" I don't know why I'm surprised. A lot of femmes fatales have daughters. Marlene Deitrich did, for instance.

"She came down from Connecticut and handled things. She had dealt with all the business papers before she called me. All clean and organized."

"Did she die here?" I ask, quietly.

He nods.

"How?"

"She didn't come down one morning to get her paper, so the manager checked. He says he's always alert to any changes in pattern, with so many older people here. She died sometime the day before—she was dressed but she'd lain down to rest, maybe felt ill. Anyway, peaceful."

His fair face is flushed. Alex, whose business depends on death, doesn't like it mentioned. I take my suitcase to the bedroom. Sharon has folded up the coverlet and stripped the pillowcases off the pillows and is stowing them into one of the trash bags she uses for linens. The headboard—padded satin—leans against the wall with the bed pulled away from it. When the Kussrows lift off the mattress, we can see, through the box spring, a pair of high heeled pumps. She took them off and died, I think, but I don't say it.

Sharon adds them to her sack of footwear. "Nearly all the shoes were in shoe bags, dustless, perfect," she says. "Everything just so."

I squat down to pull the books out of the bedside table, since they'll want to take that soon. I load them into the suitcase. They are mostly current hardcovers, only one or two vintage.

Hank comes back in and edges the vanity out from the wall. "Comes apart," he says. "Piece of cake."

Sharon says she'll have it empty shortly. He stands there for a minute, adjusting his weightlifting belt, then says, "Wife died three years ago."

Sharon looks up at him.

He tugs his iron gray forelock. "Got my own hair and"—he clacks—"all my teeth. How'd you like to go to dinner sometime? I'll buy you a steak."

Sharon says, "Oh, I don't think so, Hank."

"No harm in asking," he says, and goes out with the bedframe.

There's a pause. I say: "What is he? 75?"

Sharon says, "In Miami, once a woman is over 50, she's supposed to go out with 80 year olds. It's a tough market."

I shake my head, but it's true. She is—in ninth grade in 1963—I figure 57. I'm 63 and I never looked at her that way. But I haven't been looking at anyone much of late except pretty gals forever young on paper. Last week I was smitten with a Broadway actress from the early '20s and then I realized she would be 105 if she weren't already dead.

"My ex-husband has a 38-year-old girlfriend," she says.

"Does he have all his teeth and hair, though?"

She laughs. "No."

Mainly to change the subject I say, "You know, what you said before, that would be a good name for a business: The Noir Boudoir. That stuff is big on Lincoln Road, things from that period, marabou slippers and dresser sets."

She says, "I have some vintage cosmetics and compacts and so on, which I haven't put on-line."

"Cast some glamour on them and maybe you can get more. Anyway, it's a memorable name."

"You want it?" she says, casually.

"No," I say. "Not at all. Your idea." Punctilious as always, we go back to work.

When I'm done, I stop by Alex in the living room, now cleared of furniture other than his chair. I tell him what I think my haul is worth to me and write him a check. He doesn't dicker; he knows I know he's seen everything I have. I cart my stuff out and then come back up to do a trip for Sharon, carrying down some garment bags and hatboxes to her car. When I leave, the old guy is filling a carton with part-used cleaning products from under the sink, and Hank and Jeff are moving the dressing table base, murmuring to each other. I ride down after them. It's hot outside, well up in the 80s. I take a moment to check on the dog, but he looks fine. There's a bowl of water on the floor of the passenger side in the shade. He's got short white hair, a barrel chest and thin bare legs. I put him down for some sad mix of terrier and chihuahua.

***

Somewhere the newspapers that reported on the death of William Dorsett may be intact. Everything is still on paper somewhere, that's my theory. But not where it's supposed to be, at the library or the newspaper's morgue. Microfilm and scanning keep the text but not the context. The juxtapositions of facing pages, the ads, the color process, the smell of the paper itself, are gone, and with them a lot of the meaning. Still I put in some time at the library on Wednesday, getting a headache from the smell of the microfiche baking as I read what I can find.

In February 1963, William Dorsett's horse, Panama Sailor, had been ailing, putting in poor times at practice. On a Saturday at Hialeah Park, Dorsett went to the stables to check whether he'd have to scratch him from a race that afternoon. Or at least so he'd said to several people in the clubhouse, where he left the Mrs. in full view of many.

In the stables, running to where they heard sounds of distress, a pair of stable boys found him, bleeding from his stomped-on head and chest, the vet there trying to calm the horse. The vet said he had been treating the horse, at Dorsett's behest, and when the owner came into the stall it had gone loco. The horse's right foreleg was badly smashed, and they had to put him down.

Between editions the cops must have sweated the vet, Dr. Lucas M. Pryor. Because now he told a different story: on Dorsett's orders he'd been doping the horse. Panama Sailor's "ailment" was a ploy to help the odds. The horse was fit and then some. He was supposed to "recover" and win—but the scheme backfired on Dorsett. This was crime but the death itself, Pryor insisted, was accidental.

There it sat till the trial. In the interim the newspapers dug into Mrs. D.'s first husband, also a William, this one called Billy Hogarth. The Hogarths were down for the winter in 1954, from Pittsburgh. Dorsett was from Ligonier, horse country, not right next door to Pittsburgh but both Western Pennsylvania. So Mr. and Mrs. Billy Hogarth could have known Dorsett, but that was unconfirmed. On March 2, 1954, Billy Hogarth, having had some cocktails, was walking back to his hotel, crossing Collins Avenue mid-block, when he was struck and killed by a 1950 Studebaker belonging to one Roy Robineau. Robineau got out after he hit Hogarth and readily admitted he was drunk. Being drunk was its own excuse then, not a crime the way it is today. The 1950 Studebaker had the distinctive "bullet nose" front end which hit Billy Hogarth just right—or just wrong. Young Mrs. Hogarth was having her hair done at the hotel salon, in honor of a party they were going to that night.

By the trial's opening reporters had gotten Helena's original name, Helen Immerton. A songbird from Kentucky—some implication of trashiness about Kentucky can be picked up even on microfiche—right across from Cincinnati. She'd sung with a band in Cincy and on live Ohio radio some in the '40s under the name Helena Merton, or possibly Martin—it was printed both ways in different editions. She married Billy Hogarth in 1948 and had a daughter and all was well till Billy Hogarth intersected with Robineau's front end. Dorsett married the pretty widow in 1955. She was 27, and 35 when she was tragically—the papers invariably appended "tragically"—widowed again. Nothing much was said about the daughter. She'd been away at school. Age 12, but the rich ship them off young, and she was a stepdaughter. One columnist mentioned Roy Robineau not being locatable, rumored to have moved out west.

Between the lines, I imagined how hard the cops worked to find a connection between Dr. Pryor the vet and the lovely Helena Dorsett, shown in photos from various social events, jaunty in sports clothes and shapely, but never vulgarly so, in evening wear. There were frequent references to their house on Leucadendra Drive, which clearly meant something about class and money. Dorsett looked handsome and strong-jawed, like an ad for aristocracy, and Dr. P. had the heavy glasses of the period and a crew cut, and that's about all you could tell about them from the microfiche. Everyone looked middle-aged in 1962.

The vet never implicated her. She testified that she had no idea of anything untoward in Mr. Dorsett's horse breeding and racing "hobby." But some dirt on her husband came out, a complaint the defense had found about a misrepresented horse he sold someone in Ligonier, which tended to support the doctor's story, but that didn't mean there hadn't been a falling out between them. So Dr. P. got second-degree murder. He went away to state prison for fifteen to twenty years—maybe a lot for second-degree, but they'd loaded on some other charges about tampering and prescriptions. Took away his vet's license, of course.

And Helen(a), née Immerton, aka Merton/Martin, Hogarth Dorsett, twice widowed, presumably sold the house on Leucadendra Drive, and moved, perhaps straight into the Delphi, who knows? On her inheritance she lived long and wore fine clothes and tried out drinks from the *Esquire Book of Cocktails* and played cards and did crosswords and died on her satin bedspread at 77. What's so tragic about that?

***

When I get home, I tell myself I need to buckle down. In the dining room, which is my workroom (I usually eat in the living room in front of the TV), I have stacked boxes full of papers I've picked up: the billing records from long-gone businesses and vintage department store ads and menus and greeting cards and falling apart old children's books and what have you. Take them apart and shuffle them up and chunk an assortment into a Ziploc and there you go: Ephemera Samplers. Very popular with scrapbookers who come by my booth on Lincoln Road on Sundays. This scrapbooking fad has raised interest in everything with old typeface or illustration. My samplers let me get rid of things of little value, though I find I go too slow because I get interested, wondering when they served broiled grapefruit as an appetizer at the Senator Hotel and setting that menu aside to keep, which is defeating my purpose.

I've got the lovely Helena's picture on the sideboard where I can see my femme fatale. Her photo has that strong line between light and shadow they liked in the '40s. Call it noir or chiaroscuro, it's dramatic. She seems a hard, lovely woman. But this isn't getting me anywhere. I assign myself to sit still and make at least two dozen Ephemera Samplers.

I jump at the phone when it rings.

It's Alex Sterling, asking if I can come meet him at Café Nublado—near his house and not that far from mine—to discuss something. "Sounds serious," I say, and he says it is, so I allow as how I'll tear myself away from work and drive down to see him.

Café Nublado is Spanish for coffee with clouds. They do the usual Cuban coffee and guava pastries, but to compete with the high-end espresso chains the walls are painted with idealized piles of cumulonimbus and the house specialty has a soft puffy topping you have to suck through to get any caffeine. Whatever happened to Sanka, I like to grumble, but the girl knows me and gives me a decaf skim Nublado.

Alex Sterling is in one of the big wicker planter's chairs out back, wearing chinos and a well-cut yellow shirt. I see he's looking worried, so I forego small talk. "What gives?"

"Somebody has burgled Sharon," he says. "She called me."

"Is she all right?"

"She's upset, naturally. The police came and took a report, but I thought you might advise her on security. I told her I'd ask you. And then—"

I wait. He wanted to meet here, not at Sharon's, so he must have something in mind.

"Do you think," he says, "I overlooked something yesterday?"

"At the Delphi?"

"She says the things they took were from there. I'm wondering if someone knew about something of great value and got it."

"But you'd looked it over—"

"Meticulously. It all seemed clean and organized. I didn't find anything hidden. But I didn't search every square molecule of space."

"I think you're as thorough as anyone could be. Did you go through the flour and sugar?"

He grins. "She didn't have any flour. I doubt she ever baked. And her sugar was lump."

"Really," I say, admiringly. "You never see that anymore, lump sugar. But you obviously looked. How 'bout the salt shaker?"

He shakes his head. "What would be in there?"

"Diamonds?"

"You're teasing me, Ray."

"Somewhat," I say. "Anyway, what Sharon had was from the bedroom. And you'd been through that."

"Yes. And Sharon says she didn't find anything concealed. Did you?"

"Well, I haven't gone through every page of every book. She could have used a thousand dollar bill as a bookmark. I'll be sure to check."

Alex says, "What I don't like is the idea that it could be one of the people who was there yesterday, who spotted something and then burgled Sharon to get it."

"Wouldn't be me. I was in the bedroom alone enough, I could have taken anything then."

"I know," he says. "And you were a policeman." Alex always says policeman, as in Say hi to the nice policeman. "Couldn't you maybe figure out what it was and who took it? If it was someone on our team."

"Tall order." I finish my Nublado. I want a cigarette but I had one an hour ago.

"Yes," he says. "But you could try, Ray, couldn't you?"

I shrug. "Well, let's go see."

He pulls out his phone and calls to say we're on our way.

So I drive us over to Sharon's place, also not far from Café

Nublado. We people with a taste for old things are clustered in the neighborhoods of Miami's Upper Eastside, where the houses were built in the '30s of cinderblock and stucco, in styles they're now calling Mediterranean Revival and Masonry Vernacular. I'm in Aqua Marina. Sharon lives in Belle Meade. Alex used to live there, but recently he cashed in and moved into a fixer-upper in Palm Grove, west of Biscayne Boulevard, for a long time the western frontier on realtors' maps. Lately people good at restoration like Alex have hopped the line in search of fun and profit there.

On the way he tells me he keeps nothing of great value in his house. He has safe deposit boxes at several banks. He adds that Mrs. Dorsett's daughter made clear that her mother's real jewelry had been in *her* safe deposit. What remained was mostly costume. I ask what the daughter was like.

"Like a respectable woman from Connecticut. She was organized and I think she knew the status of her mother's estate in advance. No nonsense. I just don't see what it could be," he muses.

Sharon comes outside as we pull up. Unadorned, wearing a white tee shirt and leggings, with her hair pulled back, she is a smaller woman than I'd thought. Perhaps she puffs herself up and puts on beads when she's working with us guys to hold her own.

She shows us where they came in. They simply bashed in window glass by the back door to the Florida room, reached in, and twisted the knob. The alarm went off, of course, as soon as the door opened, but—as I'm telling her—there's a limit to alarm systems. "The noise is useless. Neighbors won't stir to take a look. The important factor is the signal through your phone line to the alarm company, who call your house in case you set it off yourself and can give them the secret code to revoke the alarm. If you don't answer, *then* they call the cops, and the cops have to get here, so this kind of thief can have a good ten-twelve minutes. A real pro will take out your phone line. What you have here is someone looking to smash and grab, probably kids wanting something to hock for drugs."

Sharon says, "But if so, why didn't they take the portable TV right here in the Florida room near the door?"

She leads us down a hall to the back bedroom she runs her business from. The intruder definitely went out of his way to get to this room.

"Forgive the mess in here," she says.

Of course, it looks far better than my place on a good day. Garments fill a chrome clothing rack, each hanger tagged with notes. Along the opposite wall a long table holds a computer, scanner, postal scale, and a piece of blue velvet with a desk lamp aimed at it, set up for photographing smaller objects. Open trash bags piled on and around an old couch under the windows are the only disorderly note. Heavy shades darken the room. I look behind them—jalousie windows, old thick glass, hard to break.

"Did you have your digital camera here?" says Alex.

"I'd been using it to shoot clothes outside, in sunlight—I hang them from my grapefruit tree. Afterward, I put it in the bedroom. It's still there."

"So what did they take?" I ask. Like Sharon, I say "they" even though I'm assuming it's a "he."

"I've made a list. The police want one and my insurance will too, but I don't think it's going to be enough for my deductible." She picks up a pad. "Shoes, clothes, linens."

"Which shoes?" asks Alex.

"Not the nicest ones." She opens the closet's pocket door and reveals shoe racks. "I'd put the best away in here. I guess they never opened this. They just got a couple of pairs of day shoes, some blouses that were here on the arm of the couch, things I was setting aside to take to the women's shelter. The women always need clothes, especially for job interviews, work. Well, they took that whole pile. Oddly, they took the satin pillowcases but not the bedspread. I think some of the makeup and perfume is gone. They spilled some powder, see?"

"Young transvestites in the neighborhood?" I say.

Alex gives me an amused look. "Yes, probably."

I say, "Most likely, they used the pillowcases to carry the other items. That's common."

"Well, it breaks up the set," Sharon says, pointing to the spread, which looks much less elegant in here, I notice.

"Had you gone through everything from the estate before the break-in?" I ask.

"Not really. I hung up all the finest clothes when I got home, to keep them nice. And then I was tired, and my daughter and her family took me out for sushi. In the morning, I went out to the post office to ship things—I try to go early every Monday, Wednesday, Friday so I don't get behind."

"So someone seeing you leave with packages would assume you'd be gone a while?"

"I suppose. I was gone about 45 minutes. When I came back the police were here, and I turned the alarm off."

"Wasn't there costume jewelry?" asks Alex.

"Yes." Sharon pulls out a vanity case from the closet floor. "It's mainly brooches, substantial ones that looked good on her suits."

She opens a jewelry roll on the blue velvet piece and snaps on the light and they shine: fake pinwheels and starbursts.

"She wore the pearl one on Sundays," I say.

"It's good," says Sharon. "Miriam Haskell."

"There was a decent coral one," says Alex, "set in 14 carat gold, which I have. The rest was costume, which is Sharon's territory."

"Any missing?"

They shake their heads.

"Well," I say, "first thing to do is fix the window. And I think you need a key-only deadbolt on that door—no reason to make things easy for them. I can do that for you, if you'd like."

"Thank you, Ray," she says, and gives me a big smile. She takes us into the living room, a quiet space in greens and beiges. One end is nearly empty. A low table holds candles and a mat is unrolled in front of it on the pickled pine floor. She sees my glance. "I do meditation," she says. "To calm down."

"Does it help?" I ask.

"Yes. You should try it, sometime. It's good for your blood pressure. You tune in to yourself and just notice what there is: the light and little sounds."

"I think I've done it," I say, "on stakeout." I'm looking at her, recognizing that after—what? three years?—I don't know her at all.

***

Driving home, I tell Alex it's impossible to say what the burglary was all about. It might be something to do with the Dorsett estate or completely random. I drop him at his house in Palm Grove, telling him I'll stay in touch with Sharon, in case she notices anything else. And otherwise keep my eyes open.

And for the next few days, I do, with no particular idea what I'm getting at. I go back to help Sharon out, but she hasn't made any further discoveries. At home, I work through all of Helena Dorsett's books and papers. The oldest thing of interest is a vintage book on how to dress, from 1939; she was still a girl, if she got it new. There are pencil tick marks next to various tips. A strawberry blonde should not wear orange reds, but blue reds and true violets. There is a chapter about shopping that tells what kind of coat to have if you can only afford one and then what to buy when you can purchase a second.

I have many pictures of Hialeah Park on postcards and programs. I went to closing day, back in 2001, and bought up a few future collectibles. It was a sad occasion. Even the pink flamingoes on their little island looked faded. I take a drive over there on Friday and circle around behind to see the area of extensive decaying stables where people used to board horses for the season. I forget what I last read about plans to reopen the track.

Then I drive on down to Coral Gables and tour Leucadendra Drive and spot the house. It's certainly worth a million now. But whatever it was worth in 1962 was plenty.

***

I think I hear someone scrabbling outside my sun porch, late Friday night, but I've had problems with possums there, getting in under the house, and anyway it might just have been palmettos chipping at the window as they do. You have to prune here constantly. I get up, turn on some lights, patrol, see nothing, and go back to bed. I take out the phone book and look her up: an H. Dorsett is listed at the right address.

Now I'm fully awake, so I go into my linen closet, full of reference books. I have a half dozen assorted Social Registers I've picked up. In the one for Greater Miami 1955 I find DORSETT, MR. AND MRS. WILLIAM ELSFORD *(Helena M. H.)* are listed at the address on Leucadendra Drive, Coral Gables. Then:

Summer: Little Chestnut Farm, Ligonier, PA
Miss Diana Hogarth

Clubs: Riviera (CG); Princeton (Miami); Rod and Reel (MB); Jockey. Clubs, Mrs: Opera Guild.

Coll, Mr: Princeton

Yacht: "Sea Lark"

I note that she chose the initial of her stage name, and then Hogarth's—which was needed to indicate where Miss Diana came from. No Coll for the Mrs. was not all that unusual in those days. I presume the Opera Guild interested her due to her musical background.

I look up Dr. Pryor, but I don't suppose veterinarians were society people. Nor is there any Roy Robineau. I don't have a register from the early '50s, but I know the Hogarths wouldn't be in there—they were staying at a hotel, not a home or a club. I put Mr. Billy Hogarth down as a young guy with a little family money, not in Mr. William Dorsett's league.

I think about money and Florida. When I first visited, years ago, after my divorce, looking to have some fun and cheer up, I was amazed to see how much money lived here, filtering in from all over America as people cashed in their piles. I cannot completely explain the fascination of discovering where they all went. In my old town when I was growing up there were some rich people. You knew who they were; you worked for them. Then they deserted, and a lot of the people in the middle left. After they made me chief, I put in a few years at my top salary and then deserted too. I bought myself a little house in a bayside neighborhood that was turning around and added my bit to the comeback. Here, I got interested in life's cast-off paper, and started to buy and sell and learn the worth of the worthless.

***

Sunday morning early, I'm at the Lincoln Road Antiques & Collectibles Market. The humidity has lifted and it's cool, in the upper 50s at 8 a.m., though it promises to warm up later. I'm in my usual spot on Drexel just off Lincoln near the community church—the side street gets morning shade. I have set up my tent with plastic side flaps. Rain—even a stiff breeze—can do a lot of damage to my stuff. But it doesn't look like bad weather today, so I leave them rolled up. I get to work, unpacking the rubber tubs of pages organized by subject, and the display rack for the intact magazines. I never dismantle anything that's perfect. Boxes of books go on the ground, and my best stuff under glass on the back table.

Other dealers pass by, circulating—we check out each other's stuff early. Sometimes an item has changed hands twice before the average buyer comes out looking. There's interest in my 1934 *Vanity Fair* with the Albert Einstein paper doll page: mint. I have it encased in plastic, but dealers know better than to touch. No one buys. I don't expect it; I've set the price high because I don't really want to let it go. When I have things laid out, I stand and stretch and look around. The Kussrows, as usual, have the corner of Drexel and Lincoln, across from where the SPCA has its table and pen of dogs up for adoption. Jeff and Hank are angling their stuff to best advantage: a bunch of Heywood-Wakefield chairs, a dresser, and there's Helena's dressing table with the circular mirror, catching and reflecting the morning sun like a fat full moon.

Sharon arrives, as promised, bringing me coffee, the Starbucks version of Nublado decaf skim, lacking the Cuban depth. While I was putting in her deadbolt on Thursday, she said she'd take me up on sharing my space and see how she did selling some things, as a start on the Noir Boudoir idea. Covering one side table with a vintage cloth, she lays out an assortment of compacts, old lipstick cases, and evening bags. I have the other side table and the back table, making a U the customer can walk into and browse. We'll sit at the outer ends in lawn chairs I brought. She's wearing her amber, which I now think of as her chest guard, and heavy tortoiseshell vintage shades. "You look invincible," I tell her, but she shakes her head.

The old guy comes by with his doggie on a leash. The pooch is wearing an argyle vest this morning, though the old guy himself is his usual shambles. He nods at us and heads for the Kussrows.

I ask Sharon to watch my stuff while I go chew the fat.

The old guy is running his hand across the dresser top. "What is this, Jeff," he asks, "mahogany?"

"Veneer," says Jeff. "In great shape. No label, but it's got the look and the lines."

The dog jumps up on the vanity bench and looks inquiringly at himself in the mirror.

"Gorgeous day," I say to all and sundry.

"Finally some fresh air," Hank says, and takes a deep breath to show off his chest expansion. He's looking in Sharon's direction.

I say, "You guys hear Sharon got burgled?"

Jeff nods. "Alex mentioned it. They get anything valuable?"

I shrug. "Just some assorted duds from that estate we did. She's mostly upset that anyone came in. Probably someone who saw her unloading."

"That's what you get when you run your business from your home," Hank says.

I say, "I've always counted on no one thinking I've got anything. House doesn't look like much, you know. Probably the least improved property in Aqua Marina at this point. You guys have a warehouse, right? Design District?"

"Right above there, Buena Vista," says Hank.

"It's a fortress," Jeff says. "We all move in when there's a hurricane. Where I live on the beach they evacuated twice this fall, for nothing, really."

Hank says, "But if a big one came, we'd be safe in there."

"Well, looks like we're through with that this year. Weather's changed." I stretch. "I'm going down to Islamorada and fish. Think I'll head down this afternoon against the traffic coming back from the Keys, take a few days."

"You got a boat?" says Hank.

"Just a small one. Boston Whaler. Sixteen feet. How long have you lived down here?" I ask Hank, now that we're talking.

"I grew up here," he says. "But I lived in Southern California for a while—used to surf, loved the beaches. Then got married, had a family, brought them back here. Got Jeff and two more you haven't met, not in the business."

Customers are talking to Jeff, who has them around behind the dressing table to show how the mirror connects. The little pooch apparently got an overblown sense of himself from his time with the mirror, because he jumps off and yanks the leash from the old guy's hand and runs across to the SPCA gang, an assortment of biggish dogs who look like they could eat him for brunch. He growls at them from his side of their not very secure-looking pen. I go over and pick him up. His little body is vibrating with indignation or machismo or whatever it is. "You've got guts," I say. I hand him back to the old guy, who takes the leash with a shaky old hand.

"Archie, say thank you," he instructs, and the dog yaps at me in what doesn't sound like gratitude.

"You should get a dog, Ray," he tells me, nodding at the orphans up for adoption.

"I probably could use a watchdog, at that. The alarm system's got a bunch of gaps, window wires rusted," I say.

The old guy walks with me back to my booth. The dog sniffs around Sharon's ankles and the old guy peruses our goods while Guillermo comes up with a heavy bundle he sets down by my chair.

Guillermo unwraps his find, a vintage interest calculating machine with Bakelite keys. "In operating condition," he boasts.

"Seriously outmoded," I say.

"But," he says, "the guys who have outmoded it love these. I had three manual typewriters in my shop and last month they all sold to high tech guys who like to decorate their offices with them."

"You never know." I say. "Business been good, then?"

"It runs hot and cold. I'm going over there to open up now."

"I could never stand being stuck in a shop all day myself," I say. And I tell him, too, that I'm going fishing, but he just shakes his head at my laziness. I let him leave a stack of cards for his shop on my table.

The little dog is nosing through my bin of Ephemera Samplers. I pull him away. "You looking for anything special this morning?" I say to the old guy. "I've got more at home, things that came from the Dorsett estate. Nice stuff."

"Just giving the dog some exercise," he says, and shuffles off.

"How old is he?" whispers Sharon.

"Too old to ask even you out," I say. She gives me a look through her shades.

And so the morning passes pleasantly. I sell *Chafing Dish Cookery* and some other '60s product brochures to a man from New Jersey who tells me about the soda fountain in his basement. Beautiful girls come by to look at Sharon's display. One buys a powder box, another an old *Vogue*. Several select the brooches and hankies and hats of Helena Dorsett, fragments of another woman's beauty, now theirs. We see a couple buy the dressing table, the fellow writing a check while the young lady sits on the bench, laughing up at him.

"I wonder if she kept it because it was a magic mirror," Sharon muses. "Maybe it showed her always beautiful and young."

"I think to her it stood for class," I say. "Some idea she'd formed of what she'd have and when she got it she never let it go. Why did she keep that whole room like that?"

Sharon shrugs. A collector comes back twice before finally buying my Albert Einstein. "That's how it works," I say to Sharon. "If you want something too much, you'll pay any price."

She says we are all poisoned by desire and tells me some more about meditation. We discuss mindfulness and the radiance of things. It gets warm by noon, and Sharon breaks out a mini-battery operated fan and fusses that the heat will ruin the perfumes. I agree with her by one that it's time to pack it in.

***

Late in the afternoon I get the Whaler out: Paper Boat, I named it. Hook the trailer to my car, drive it over to the marina on the Little River, and leave the boat and trailer there, for a fee. Driving back through my neighborhood, I take a different route and park a few blocks down beyond my house. I stroll back, enjoying the air, and think how I really have to walk more.

Home, I turn off the alarm system and settle down for a night of meditation. It's after 1 a.m. when I see a flashlight flicker by the dining room window. For God's sake, break in by the back door, I think. That window frame is rotting from the rainy season and needs to be replaced. I left the bolt unlocked.

He works his way back there. A short smash of glass, and he's in: sun porch, kitchen. He's taking his time. He must be thanking his stars there's no alarm. He slows down. In the dining room: his flashlight circles the piles on the table, and then he sends a beam into the living room towards my feet. I turn on the standing lamp by my chair and the old guy blinks at me.

I say, "Where'd you leave the dog?"

"Home," Cash says.

"What are you looking for?"

He tries to shrug, the big robber: "Anything of value."

"No," I say. "You're looking for something about you—or you and her. Which one are you? Robineau or the vet?"

"Lucas Pryor. As you say, the vet."

"Lucas turned into Cash?"

"No one ever called me Lucas much," he says. "Newspapers always use your formal name. I got the nickname as a boy because other kids were always hitting me up for small loans and I was generous. You wouldn't think it now, I realize."

"You killed the second husband," I say.

Sadly he says, "And I killed the horse."

"Well, you served your time," I say. "Can't be tried twice. So it wasn't that she had evidence. It was—"

He pulls a gun from the pocket of his droopy shorts.

"Oh Jeez," I say. "I've got one too." And I show him my Glock. "Yours looks rusty." It's a Jennings J-25, dregs of the gun world. The finish is gone on it. "Ever shot it?"

He shakes his head and lowers the gun, some. His hand is trembling so much I'm afraid he's going to shoot me accidentally. Those pistols jam a lot, but every once in a while one manages to emit a bullet. I say, "Sit down and let's talk."

He takes the chair across from me, propping his gun-holding hand on its broad arm.

I hold my Glock in my lap, ready if needed, hoping it won't be.

He says, "You were expecting me."

I nod. Though to be honest I'd also worked out a theory where Hank Kussrow was Robineau.

I say, "I figure you killed her. Are you looking for something you touched when you did it? Something that might have your fingerprints that you couldn't explain? Maybe this?" I point to the picture in the Lucite frame, on the table beside me. "Did you expect Sharon to have it?"

"You don't understand," he says.

"I probably don't. What was it all for? You killed Dorsett for her?"

"She needed him dead."

"Oh," I say. "Did she ask you?"

"She . . . implied it."

"Why'd she need him dead?"

"She said Dorsett was a bully. And a killer. She told me that he'd seen her when she and her first husband came to Miami Beach. And he wanted her, naturally. But she was married with a child. And then someone ran her husband down and she was a widow, so when Dorsett courted her, she married him. It was only after—years after—that she found out that he'd hired the man who hit her husband. This is what she told me, you understand?"

"Dorsett hired Robineau?"

"She said that when she expressed a desire to leave Dorsett, he told her so and frightened her."

"And Robineau, what happened to him?"

"She said Dorsett took him out on his yacht and drowned him, in the Bahamas somewhere."

"More death by transportation," I say.

"It's not funny."

"So she told you all this, and you decided you could take him on, this brute?"

He shifts his jaw and nods.

"She was worth killing for?"

"You should have seen her. At the racetrack, in blue linen. She was a dream. Then Dorsett asked me whether I could make it seem that the horse was having problems, to jigger the odds. So I did that, God help me. He was, as she said, a bully—he bullied me, never knowing what I was thinking. I stopped doping Panama Sailor in time for him to run. That was the plan. But on race day I gave the horse a little something else and Dorsett handled him rough and the horse knocked him down and I . . . helped."

"And then you didn't tell."

"I kept my mouth shut for her," he says.

"Did she ask you to?"

"We only had a moment," he says. "At the stables. She came in after he was dead. They let her see his body, but then she asked to see the horse, and I was in with Panama Sailor, trying to fix his leg but it was no good. She said, 'Thank you, Cash,' which they might think was thanks about the horse. After that, we couldn't speak again because the cops had me."

I say, "You hadn't slept with her?"

"Oh," he says. "I had. She was a dream, I told you. Your loveliest, dirtiest dream."

I'm thinking that's a quote from somewhere, but I'm not sure.

"Did you think if you killed him you'd keep her?"

"I didn't think that much. I felt she was a creature in trouble and I would get her out. The police took me in right after I put the horse away, and after that all I could do was try to keep her out of the story."

"You're an idealist," I say. "You could have cut a deal and given her to the law."

"I was an idealist," he says. "Certainly so."

"And when you got out of prison, you didn't look her up?"

"No," he says, "I stayed away."

"Why?"

"Well, prison broke me, I suppose you'd say. I didn't do well there. I loathe violence." He clears his throat, his sandy old voice wearing out. "When I got out, I hated that I'd killed, and I didn't want to see her or for her to see me. I couldn't earn a living as a vet, just did odd jobs and picked up money and lived close to the ground and tried to recuperate. You could live cheaply here then. I've been over ten years in Palm Grove. I'm just down the street from Alex. It cost very little, till lately. They're about to redo my building now, but for years it was full of poor folks. Nobody bothered us, Archie and me, because we didn't have anything worth taking, as you said this morning about your house. When you were implying you had something I'd want."

I ignore that. "Okay, so you steered clear of her. Then?"

"About a month ago, we did a job at the Delphi, somebody downsizing to a nursing home. You weren't there. Just Jeff and Hank. I was lugging stuff out for Alex, and she saw me. She caught me outside when I was alone and asked me to come see her."

"Did you recognize her?"

"She hadn't changed nearly as much as I had. And she recognized me." He clears his throat. "In prison I learned to think more—what would be the word—more cunningly. And I had thought about her story." He gives a dry smile. "Often. As you can imagine."

"Yes, I can."

"I kept seeing patterns. I killed the second husband, somebody killed the first for the second. The guy who killed the first got killed—at least that's what she'd said. It could be simpler, I felt. I did it for her. So maybe the others did it for her."

"Wait. Robineau killed Hogarth for her?"

"Could have been. Could have been just because Dorsett paid him, but I looked up what I could find and he hadn't been a bad guy, just a silly rich drunk. So I think he may have done it for her, yes, sir."

"And Dorsett killed Robineau?"

"For her, I think. I mean, at her behest. Possibly."

"And you killed Dorsett."

"Indisputably. So, if you pay attention to the pattern, someone ought to kill me. I'm the loose end. She could have been looking for me, but I would have been hard to find. I'd entered the cash economy. I have no phone. And maybe she just didn't have a man to sic on me."

"Well, maybe," I say.

"I don't have a lot of evidence," he says. "But she said she was happy to see me. Now, should she have been happy?"

"Well, you'd been a stand-up guy and gone to jail without ratting on her. You might have been her idea of a hero," I say, though I know he's right.

He shakes his head. "But I could still have sent her to prison, now."

"Could you? She knew you were going to kill her husband?"

"She asked me to do it, in the clearest way one could without saying it right out."

"In bed, was it?"

"In bed. Her bed. I have no evidence for that. But if I were to say she had done so, even now, would the police not at least speak to her?"

"They're not that eager to open settled cases from 1963."

"But there could be scandal, and she'd become respectable again. And she might think the police would care. My impression was that she was scared that I'd appeared in her building."

"Okay. Let's say you're right. She should've avoided you. Instead, what did she do?"

"She wanted to get together, she said. I agreed to see her, but said I had a lot of work." He laughs his dry laugh. "So we made the date for a week from then. I was to come to her place, have a drink, then maybe we'd go out to dinner. I wanted the week to think. What would she do with the loose end? She'd be looking for a way to kill me, I felt. She had to. I considered running, but she would be able to find me now. People can't disappear as easily as they used to. So I put on my jacket and tie, left my dog with plenty of food and water and the door ajar in case I didn't come back, and went to see her."

He's caught up in his story and no longer actually holding the gun, I notice.

"When I got there I was scared. She offered me a cigarette, but I don't smoke anymore. Offered me a Manhattan, which I accepted, but didn't drink, just lifted it to my lips and put it down. My dog, Archie, has quite a few ailments. I had a dog tranquilizer with me to put in her drink, but I didn't get a chance. Her eyes were on me all the time." He sighs. "I was raised to think of women as emotional creatures."

"Creatures?"

"Weren't you? Soft, dependent, lacking calculation. Of course, that's a mistake we make about many other creatures, too, underestimating them. In her case, believe me, she was rational, detached. Watchful. She said she'd thought about me, a lot. That she'd been alone a long time. And she invited me into the bedroom. Perhaps I was supposed to be woozy. I know I was shaky, anyway, following her in."

"My God," I say, "that bedroom."

"She lay back on the bed, against the pillow, the same way she had when—" He clears his throat. "And I sat beside her and leaned forward, and then I pressed the other pillow over her face."

"Didn't she fight you?"

"She died unexpectedly fast. I was thinking she'd pass out and then I would give her an empty injection, just put some air into her vein and cause an embolism."

"You had a hypodermic on you?"

"I have a whole kit. You know you can buy anything in Miami. But she just stopped breathing. She must have had a heart attack—perhaps the shock?"

"She was old."

"And she smoked," he says. "She may have had heart disease. I figured nobody pays attention to the death of an old lady in her own bed. I took off her shoes, and wiped them, and set them on the floor. I wanted it to look like she'd felt ill and had to lie down and then died. I cleaned up the glasses, dried them, put them away. I have them now. I got them from the kitchen when we were there. I believe I have washed them half a dozen times. In with her liquor, there was a medicine bottle with a dropper. Maybe it was bitters, maybe something else. I took it with me and later threw it into the bay, then realized I should have kept it, had it tested if I needed to prove self-defense. I left her one cigarette butt in the ashtray. I wiped whatever I thought I'd touched. But I was fairly sure we'd be in there to do the estate clean-up and I'd handle a lot of things and so my fingerprints wouldn't mean anything." His voice rises. "I'm not going back to jail!"

"I understand," I say, soothingly. "How did you know Alex would get the estate job?"

"Alex left cards when we were there before, at the desk and by the mailboxes and so on. So I didn't think anyone would find it odd that Helena had picked one up and had it in her desk, where she had other business cards. The daughter saw it and called. It was a gamble, but a good one. I left feeling fairly confident and calm. It was only afterwards that I started to doubt myself and worry about little things. I couldn't have taken the pillow-case. That would have drawn attention. But later I kept thinking about it—forensics people can pick up tiny fibers, hairs. That day we were there I never could get into the bedroom alone till after Jeff and Hank carted off the furniture, and by then Sharon had packed up the bedclothes. I'm sorry I had to steal from her."

"What'd you do with the pillowcases?"

"I burned them both in my sink. I didn't know which one was which."

"And the rest of the stuff you took?"

"In my van. I was going to put it in a dumpster, somewhere far off."

"Sharon was going to give it to abused women."

He looks somewhat ashamed.

"Did you touch the dressing table?" I ask.

"I don't think so. But afterwards I wasn't sure."

"So on Lincoln Road you touched it and you let the dog hop up there?" He nods. "Did you touch the portrait?"

"I don't recall. There were a number of pictures in the living room that she showed me—her daughter and her grandchildren. I think it was there. I don't think I touched it. Did I?"

I say, "Lucite does hold prints. But I had already cleaned it myself when I got it home. Here—look at it. You're safe."

He takes it, holding between both palms, and I lift his pistol off the chair arm and put it on the floor beside me.

"So there's no evidence," he says.

"Just what's in your head," I say.

"I wouldn't have hurt you, Ray," he says. "Tonight, I didn't think you'd be here."

"But you brought the gun."

"I bought it from somebody I know at the flea market. I said I wanted it to defend myself. And I did. I thought if the police were to catch me breaking in at Sharon's, or here, I could use it on myself. Or wave it at them and they'd shoot me. I just don't want to go back to jail." He says it calmly this time, his eyes on me.

I think how we look, the two of us here, in our circle of light, one holding the portrait, the other the gun.

"Miami," I say. "The place is full of killers. Guys who work on your car may have been in death squads in Peru, dictators own steak houses, drug kingpins become developers. I can't fix every little thing. Go home. I know you did it, and you know I know, but there's not a bit of evidence left, I promise you. She's ash and her things are scattered and scattering further every day."

He uses his shirttails to wipe off the picture frame and hands it back to me. Her eyes smile at me in the lamplight.

"Is that how she looked when you knew her?"

"She's a little younger, but yes."

"It's driving you nuts," I say, "isn't it?"

"What is?" he says, but he knows.

"The shred of a shadow of a glimpse of a chance that she might have been innocent. That the first story was true, the one she told, with Dorsett the killer and bully and you the rescuer. The one you went to jail on."

He says, "I'm sure as one can be."

"It's just too bad you have a conscience."

He blinks at me. "She didn't," he says. And sighs. He picks up his flashlight and nods to me and leaves. I bolt the door after him. On close inspection his gun's in even worse shape than I thought. I wipe off the prints and put it into a grocery bag. I'll drop it out to sea. I listen to the sound the palmettos make chattering against my windows and treat myself to a cigarette.

***

Three weeks later, on a Friday, I'm getting spruced up to go out. Two days after our talk, Cash was found, dead, in his apartment. He had a needle beside him containing nothing but air. In a note he left his worldly goods to Alex and asked that I take care of his dog Archie. He left no explanation for his suicide other than to say, "I'm very tired."

Our team cleared out his place. He had many old books, those of most interest with illustrated plates of birds and animals. He owned a complete medical bag and a collection of antique vet instruments that Guillermo says might be worth something. These things might possibly realize enough to repay Alex for the cremation. None of us could start the van, but Alex located some of Cash's buddies from the flea market in Fort Lauderdale, and they came down and towed it away. The Kussrows declared his furniture of no resale value and we put it all out on the street for pickers to take. The building itself will soon be gutted.

Alex is looking for another trustworthy clean up man. I haven't told him about Cash. The morning after his visit to me, Sharon found the stolen clothing tossed behind her hibiscus bushes. Alex and Sharon like my theory the burglar was a boy seeking women's clothes who found them too dowdy.

Archie came to me with a list of what he eats and his ailments and a wardrobe of waistcoats and sweaters. I think Cash underestimated him. There's a nip in the November air this evening, but I'm making Archie tough it out. We'll walk down to Sharon's and take her to dinner at a new restaurant on Biscayne. We'll go afterwards to Café Nublado and beyond that, who knows? She's a warm woman, as I'm coming to appreciate.

On my way out I stop in the dining room—as I often do—
to look at the portrait of Helena Dorsett. What was it she had?
Beauty enough to kill for, any way you look at it. I strain to re-
capture the woman I met. Quite a lady, I remember thinking. Her
face is a pattern of shadow and light. Now, just paper.

Gift Wrap

This year the store, Paper, Ink, has set up a kiosk out front, in its hip block of shops, and Jen works there all day wrapping. You bring your present with your receipt from one of the stores and get a discount. It's part of the strategy for reviving this old beach town's center. She uses muted, cool, shimmery papers and French wire ribbons. She does each gift with care, choosing among the trims she made ahead—seashells and starfish sprayed silver, the Florida equivalent of snowflakes.

When she began, shoppers would watch her and then go into the store to buy supplies to do the work themselves, but now, two days before Christmas, they have abandoned such ambitions. Today some even come with presents bought elsewhere and pay full price. She is astonished at how much money other people have to throw away.

A young guy places three identical jewelry boxes on her counter. She asks how he wants her to mark which is whose. "No," he confides, "I got them all the same, ankle bracelets, no mistakes. They're for my girlfriends." He says this ruefully, with a flash of dark eyes. As she twists out a bow, he says, "You have beautiful hands," such a flirt she knows how easily he's keeping three women on the hook. She remembers when she was single and had time to be miserable.

Now she has a sweet husband, Carlos, and a son, Riley, six, so beautiful her heart twists each time she sees him. Her father has been with them since the weekend, and right about now he's picking up her sister at the airport. Her mother died last June and for the first time Jen is the home base for the holiday. Her mother made a big deal of Christmas—too big, Jen always thought, full of such effort and dressing up, no one could relax. She misses her mother, but she definitely doesn't want to be like her.

At 5:30, just as she's closing, her sister arrives. Haley is younger, taller, blonder, and richer than Jen. That's always her first impression, of Haley's vitality, before her discontent comes through. She works eighty hours a week marketing technology. Haley's phone calls are a cascade of promotions, raises, moving expenses to new states, last month a vacation to Australia.

"Dad's parking," Haley says. "Riley's with him. He's so cute. I haven't seen him since the funeral."

Jen asks Haley to help her carry in the supplies and introduces her to the other women from the shop. Haley is pleasant till they get outside again. Then she says, "Riley says you didn't make the lebkuchen."

Jen knew there would be trouble if she didn't make those cookies. Haley sent her the recipe in November, even though Jen already had it, and a set of cutters just like their mother's. "Listen, this is what we're doing," Jen says. "Carlos got this smoker and he's smoking a goose. I'm making light stuff—we're having a fruit salad and pumpkin risotto and green beans and some good bread. And mango ice cream for dessert because that's Riley's favorite. He wouldn't even eat the lebkuchen last year. He doesn't like food to be crunchy. Okay?"

"No mashed potatoes?" her sister says. "No squash?"

"No. And no minced pie."

"Okay, but there have to be lebkuchen," her sister says.

"I got the ingredients, Haley, but I just didn't have time. They take all day, you know that. I've been working extra hours, and I've had Dad here. Give me a break."

"Lebkuchen are traditional in our family," Haley says. "Our great-grandmother made them."

"Sometimes you have to start new traditions," Jen says.

Haley doesn't answer. She has a stubborn sulky look Jen knows well, the one she wore when she wanted something from their mother.

"Mom made all that stuff last year," Jen says, "when she shouldn't have."

Last year at Christmas, their mother knew she was sick. She didn't tell them till after the dinner, after the huge ridiculous turkey and mashed potatoes and creamed onions and the big sticky trifle no one ate. Last year—the sisters look at each other and veer away. Riley runs up to them, towing his grandfather.

"You're right," Haley says. But she doesn't sound convinced.

***

Jen and Carlos have a small blue deco house in an old neighborhood on the rise. It has a fireplace, a little turret, and hardly any closets. When they get home she puts her sister's two big suitcases in the narrow Florida room, where there's a futon. Her dad has been sleeping there but now he'll bunk in with Riley.

After dinner they all decorate the small tree with her collection of birds, Guatemalan and Moravian doves, origami cranes, sequined peacocks, lovebirds of spun glass. They top it with a paper partridge in a nest of gold shreds Riley made when he was with her at work after school last week. Then she lets her sister read to Riley and put him to bed.

When she goes in to kiss him goodnight, after doing the dishes, Haley is telling him how their great-grandmother came from Alsace as a small girl, her father a baker.

"Lebkuchen was their recipe," Haley says, looking at Jen. "It's from the word *lieb*, love. It means love cookie."

"Do you remember them from last year?" Jen asks him. Riley sleepily shakes his head no.

When Jen was Riley's age her great-grandmother was still alive—a hefty woman with gray braids pinned up around her head in a crown and the most wonderful cheeks, ruddy and curved. Riley's cheeks have that same shape right now. And so Jen yields. "I guess we could make them tomorrow," she says to Haley. "But you'll have to do most of the work."

***

Her dad—Frank Riley, Big Riley he wants to be called now—has gone his own way since her mother's death. Up in Newport News, he fished all summer and never cleaned the house. This week, when Jen sent him out for groceries, he found a neighborhood bar she didn't know existed, a cubbyhole where the owner, Ed, is a great guy, her dad says. They were in the same navy, same ocean. Now her dad asks if he can invite Ed for Christmas dinner. What can she say but yes? And his girlfriend, her dad adds, the barmaid, a great gal. They'll bring something to eat.

Later, as they collapse into bed, she tells Carlos it's all too much.

"Next year, Jenny," he says, "we'll find someplace to take everybody out." Carlos has always welcomed her family. His parents are long dead. As a child he was sent from Chile to be raised by his aunt, who passed away while he was in college. After her mother's death he wept in big coughing groans. For that, among other things, she's sure she'll always love him.

***

"You add the baking soda to the mix of molasses and sugar and spices and lard and it all fizzes up. That's the fun part," her sister says. Riley, in his striped pajamas, sits on a stool, watching seriously.

"Now the egg yolk. Then you sift in flour a cup at a time." Haley sifts while Jen stirs.

"I just barely remember when our great-grandmother made these," Jen says. "You were a baby then, Haley."

"The earliest I remember," Haley says, "is Grandma's house. She lived in the mountains," she tells Riley, "in a big old house."

"Everyone would gather. There were so many women—two different Aunt Mildreds, and Grandma, and Mom, and Aunt Judy who used to be married to our Uncle Bob."

"They'd put the dough in a crock and set it outside to chill overnight."

"We're going to have to put it in the fridge. God, there's a lot of it, Haley."

"And this is the half recipe—"

"It needs to chill till it's hard. And then we'll roll it out and cut it. Here are the cutters. You can play with them, Riley, they're not sharp. After you bake them and they cool, you ice them."

Her arm aching, Jen hands off to Haley, turns to make coffee. She can hear her father moving around in the bathroom. Carlos left for work early.

"So there's a story Mom told us," Haley says.

"Tell me," Riley says.

"Well, it seems that our mom and dad got engaged just before Christmas one year, and then, when all the women were making the lebkuchen, she was helping and she noticed after they'd made the dough—"

"I think it was after the rolling out," says Jen

"No, it was after making the dough, after it had been put outside and turned into a big frozen lump, as I heard it. Anyway, Mom noticed that she'd lost her engagement ring."

"This old tale," her father says as he comes into the kitchen.

"Well, they looked all over. The other women had put their rings in a teacup before they started, but Mom was so proud of her new ring, she hadn't wanted to take it off." Haley shook her arm, stretched. "And they realized it must be in the dough."

Jen takes over. The dough is almost too stiff to stir. "So they looked for it when they made the cookies, but they didn't see it," Jen says. "And then as everyone ate them, they had to be really careful because a diamond could crack your teeth, you know."

"What are you talking about?" her dad says. "Those lebkuchen are so hard they can break teeth all on their own. That's how I lost mine," he says and pops out his partial plate, to Riley's delight.

"Oh Dad," says Haley. "Just 'cause it's not your family recipe."

"My mother made fruitcake," he says. Haley and Jen roll their eyes at each other. Nobody liked that fruitcake, gummy and stiff.

"Let me finish the story," Jen says. "So guess who bit into a cookie and found it?"

"Who," says Riley. "Did you, Mom?"

"No, no, I wasn't born yet."

"Not even thought of," their dad says. "Your mother wasn't the type."

Jen and Haley laugh at their dad, the rogue.

"No, Mary found it. That's your grandmother," he says to Riley. "She ate nothing but lebkuchen all Christmas day, she was so determined not to let that ring be lost down anyone's gullet."

"Which shape cookie was it in?" asks Riley.

His grandfather looks over the Santa, the bell, the Christmas tree, the moon, the star, and the gingerbread boy. "It was in the moon. And that's why, your grandmother said, the moon always tastes the best."

***

Later, her father, alone with her, says, "You know, that bit with the ring didn't happen to your mom, but to your Aunt Judy, when she was your uncle's fiancée."

"What do you mean? Mom always told it to us this way."

"Well, as I recall it happened to Judy, and then when Judy left the family, in the divorce, I think your mother sort of adopted it. You couldn't let such a fun story go just because of a little divorce."

"I can't believe that. Really? Are you just teasing me?"

"Your mother had her ideas," he says, looking so sad all of a sudden that Jen lets it go.

***

Christmas Eve. She wraps umbrellas, diving gear, breakable bowls, designer toothbrushes, lotions with the smell of carnations and rain. People are humming, people are crazed.

She worked as a freelance graphic artist before she married Carlos, but when she got pregnant so soon and they moved into the house, she took on fewer jobs and soon hardly any clients came to her. She started the job at Paper, Ink when Riley went into kindergarten with the idea that there'd be design work involved, but all she has designed so far are invitations and announcements. She teaches card-making classes and works the counter. She has the feeling that all her indomitability, all her thought and skill, are being poured into things that don't get anywhere, don't mount up. They're like this wrapping she's doing, lavished with her talent only to be torn apart tomorrow and tossed out.

When she gets home, Carlos is drinking a beer in the back yard and watching Riley chase lizards. "She's sent me to Publix, twice," Carlos says. "On Christmas Eve. She needed more baking sheets, and then waxed paper and containers to put the cookies in, after. And I had to take the battery out of the smoke detector—it kept going off."

"I'm sorry," Jen says. "Hey Riley, how come you're not helping Aunt Haley?"

"I did," he says, "but I got tired. Look Mom, my tooth is loose." And he wiggles his lower left front tooth till it sticks out at a wild angle. Already? She feels a pang. It's all going to happen to him—loss, change, death. She knows she must be tired, to leap from a loose tooth to her son's mortality.

She gathers her strength and pushes through a wall of gingery heat into the kitchen. Haley's hair is in her face. "Your kitchen is small," Haley says accusingly.

"Hi, honey—I'll help you in a minute." Jen walks into the bedroom and closes the door. She changes into a tee shirt and shorts, pulls her hair back, and takes a deep breath before she goes out to bake.

"It must be a hundred degrees in here," Haley says, pulling a hot tray out.

"At least. Florida's no place for this kind of cooking. I told you that."

"You know what," Haley says, "I don't need this. I've been working for hours, just trying to make something nice—" Her voice breaks.

"You're just like Mom," Jen says. "You want everything to be a big production." She tries to say it lightly, but it comes out with a sting.

"I'm not the one," says Haley. "It's you. You have to have your own ideas about how everything's supposed to be, all new and different and artsy—"

"Okay, fine. At least in her own home," Jen dumps shortening on the next sheet right over the greasy crumbs, "Mom got to do things her way."

"Humph," grunts Haley, a sound so precisely like their mother in her Christmas snit that Jen wants to laugh.

And then, to her horror, as she fits lebkuchen on the baking sheet, she humphs, too. Maybe it's a German noise, she thinks, old as Father Christmas and the spice cookies themselves, an ancient female sound of solstice effort.

"It's so hard to believe she's gone," Haley says, and the sisters work on through a glaze of tears.

***

Twelve dozen cooling cookies fill the house with spice. Her dad has picked up pizza and they eat it in the yard.

Jen puts Riley to bed and almost falls asleep beside him, soothed by his even breathing. She and Carlos go about their final Christmas Eve tasks while Haley mutters over the icing. She covers the dining room table with waxed paper and lays the cookies out on it.

Jen sways, looking at her. Where does her sister get the energy?

"Go to bed," Haley says, unexpectedly tender. "I have it under control. You were right—these are too much to do."

"Maybe a quarter recipe?" Jen sticks her finger in the icing, already hardening.

"You need a team of women."

"Women who have time," Jen agrees.

***

Christmas morning is warm, shiny. Jen is the first up, leaving Carlos snoring. Her father lies in a sleeping bag by Riley's bed, surrounded by stuffed animals, with his teeth out. Riley is cuddled next to him. Haley, on the futon, is tousled, groggy, young.

Jen plugs in the lights and the tree glitters, all the birds flocked upon it, presents mounded underneath. Hers (fountain pens for the adults, an easel and art set for Riley) are wrapped in silver and purple, Carlos's done in funny papers he saved up. Haley's gifts make a pile of traditional green and red. Her father's, in foil bags, are clearly bottles. Santa—very hip—left presents wrapped in white tissue rubberstamped with hot pink reindeer. She sits enjoying the way it all shimmers until the others get up, thinking how her mother must have felt, last Christmas, trying to make something lavish before she left them.

Then, in their pajamas, her family opens everything in a binge of rip and ooh.

And the day actually goes something like she'd imagined. They hang around and play with Riley's new kangaroo and joey puppets and world habitats puzzle and the whoopee cushion from his grandfather, while the goose smokes. The rest of the dinner is easily made. Her dad's buddy Ed shows up with his girlfriend, Emilia, who brings a *paneton*, traditional, she says, at home in Lima. "Somewhat like fruitcake," her dad says, "but cakier," and then Carlos says, "It's what my aunt used to serve for dessert on Christmas, always with cocoa."

So their Christmas dessert is mango ice cream, lebkuchen, hot chocolate and *paneton*. The lebkuchen are thicker than normal. "I probably didn't roll them out enough. I was trying to go fast," Haley says.

They lack that crisp snap, but they're delicious, better in fact, altogether more southern and yielding. Jen tastes more molasses, less clove. And Riley is already halfway through a moon.

When, He Wondered

Maybe it was at the Fenwicks' playoff party in January, when Tom went to the kitchen for a beer, and Elise came up behind him as he turned in the cold exhale of the refrigerator. She said, "Was I wrong? I thought you wanted to kiss me." He heard the football shouts from Wick's den, the chattering living room, his own voice, rough with surprise, saying, "Who wouldn't?" Was it then he crossed the line?

Or there was the afternoon at the Holiday Inn Express twenty miles north, when he asked if she still did it with Wick. Elise sat cross-legged on the bed, sighed, pulled her chestnut hair up into a knot revealing her pretty ears and tiny diamond teardrops, and said she had to, that once when they had gone without for a month, for no good reason, she just hadn't felt like it, he'd hired a detective. She saw a charge she didn't recognize listed on a credit card bill, and then, in Wick's desk, she located the report, filled with daily schedules of Elise driving their daughter Nikki to school and horseback riding, and photos of Elise at a fundraiser for literacy, at the gym, standing beside Wick at a groundbreaking. Though the detective didn't find anything because there'd been nothing to find, that wasn't a risk she could take anymore, could she?

From this Tom could tell she wasn't going to leave Wick, and all Wick had, for him. He hadn't really imagined she would. But still, from then on he had to picture what she was doing to deflect suspicion.

How about when Wick asked him to go to the driving range one evening in early June? They'd shot hundreds of buckets of balls here when they were teenagers. Now their shadows stretching towards the 50-yard marker were wider, Tom's with a breadth of shoulder he hadn't had when young, and, okay, some gut. The dark green Wick shadow reached, as always, farther, his inch of height advantage multiplied by the low angle of the sun. Tom swung his three wood and listened to Wick complain. The wife, a bit extravagant, money just vanished through her fingers, and Nikki, who knew a kid could cost so much? And bigger problems, the pause in real estate sales since the winter, the sinkhole suits at Spoonbill, the loans and due dates, how overextended you could get when things were ticking down. Maybe it was time to cash it all in. But he'd need a bit of help to do that. And who else could he ask but Tom?

***

When, as young guys starting out, they worked construction together on Sunshine Marketplace, the first shopping center near Peregrine Springs, Wick hadn't liked the grubby stuff, the details of aggregate and rebar. He wanted to rise from concrete to dreams. And he did, built the outlet mall near the highway, then the hotel and conference center, the first golf condos, the Spanish-Moorish developments that ineluctably surrounded the village where they'd grown up. After twenty-three years the Sunshine Marketplace, weathered and out of style, was gutted and expanded by Wick's company, re-facaded and renamed The Shops at Spoonbill, with signs proclaiming that 600 acres of scrubland behind it would be, Coming Soon: Spoonbill, A Golf Resort Community, a Bill "Wick" Fenwick Project. Wick liked to name things Heron, Hawksbill, Manatee—evocations of what he was displacing. Wick would say that was Florida tradition: Peregrine Springs had been no place in the middle of nowhere, an imaginary paradise, when it was incorporated optimistically in the '20s. In their childhood, it had been a would-be artist town with a few motels and cottages on the Little Peregrine River. Now it was cute and clogged with cars circling to park, people lined up to grab cash at a bank machine, get coffee in the old drugstore building, and search the boutiques of the Peregrine Springs Arcade to decorate their new homes with the plunder of the world.

Wick had carried him along—Tom the supply guy, the one with the patience for measurements, quantities, invoices, Tom an essential part, Wick always said, of his success. Tom had dated fun, tan, athletic women Florida had in abundance, but somehow rather than marry he moved toward solitude. He could afford toys, Jeep and sport catamaran and dirt bike, and a golf villa that faced a fairway, across a finger of water where gators sometimes sunned. Before he moved in he'd put backstops on doors and re-vented the laundry, little things not standard in a Bill "Wick" Fenwick home where people boasted about the two-story Great Room and the terrazzo floors. On the first floor "garage and laundry level," which opened onto the lap pool and lanai, Tom installed a tool wall and workbench. He had a library with louvered shutters and a leather chair where he read with sun-dazzled eyes at the end of the day, a glass of Irish whiskey on the oak table beside him, some big book full of facts open on his lap.

Tom liked to read earth science, geology, geography, so he understood the unreliability of the landscape, the karst topography of Florida, how the ground water, slightly acidic, dissolved the calcite in the limestone as it worked its way down through, creating voids. As long as the water table stayed high enough to buoy up the overburden, your mantle of sand and clay, you had the illusion of solid ground. But when you lowered the water level, by stripping out slash pines, by digging drainage canals, by paving so the run-off was redistributed, well, sooner or later, say early one April morning, something had to give. The curve of dirt that would be the Spoonbill clubhouse drive became a bridge over nothing and then dropped, taking two trucks into the widening cavity as the first workers tossed aside their coffee and ran for it. By the time Tom got there, a crane had fallen in. He ordered everything drivable moved, but the men didn't particularly want to risk it. He found Wick standing on the roof of the Shops at Spoonbill supermarket, looking out at the catastrophe, arms crossed, jaw square, as newspapermen took pictures of him saying, truthfully, that no one could predict this, it was an act of Florida nature, unfathomable and bizarre. TV helicopters hovered as the sinkhole swallowed the foundations for half a dozen "executive homes," two of them already sold. Hungry attorneys arrived by day, and teenagers showed up at night, so you had to hire guards to keep them from drinking and daring each other to venture down into the pit. No one knew if the sinkhole would take more. Building of the Homes at Spoonbill was indefinitely suspended.

And somehow this disaster had given Wick the idea he laid out that evening at the driving range in June. The way he was going to keep what he could.

***

East of town, in the woods Tom Baugh and Bill Fenwick had roamed as boys, was one of the original "sights" of the area, a sinkhole known as Old Crater because early travelers ascribed it to a meteor, where a thousand years ago the land had collapsed to the aquifer. This sink, of course, looked nothing like the raw wound at Spoonbill. Trees that grew up out of its sides formed a canopy. The water in its depths was rumored to be bottomless, to be haunted by sacrificed Tequesta maidens or ambushed conquistadors, to be fed by pure and magical springs, to have patches of quicksand, to lead to caves in which was hidden pirate treasure.

Parents warned against swimming in Old Crater. But the boys had boundless confidence—inexplicable, now Tom thought about it—and they explored. Others before them had made a pathway through the greenery, spiraling down to the water. When they dove, they found springs, and, where there was sand, shark's teeth. Once, swimming underwater, they popped up into a cave at the western edge of the sinkhole with a ledge they could sit on, and as they watched they saw the water moved, sluggishly yes, but always southwestward.

Tom theorized that the water here might connect eventually to the Little Peregrine, that these springs might feed an underground river. "No way to know but to try," said Wick, and they filled their lungs and dove, their bodies slim darters slipping downstream, going on past caverns, possible channels, as if they knew the way, till the choice was turn back or drown, but they saw light and came up in another sink—smaller, a hole six feet across and ten feet up, its sides erose and crumbly.

"We can just dive and go back," said Tom, but Wick—and maybe this was the moment he took the lead?—found footing on an outcropping near water level, and made a stirrup with his hands, and Tom, lighter, stepped up, then stood on Wick's shoulders and hoisted himself to the edge. He grabbed on with his legs to a bush there, nothing that should have held, really, reached down, and grabbed Wick's hand, and Wick climbed right up and over him, then lifted him to the top. They stood in an overgrown spot they hadn't seen before, with the sun just overhead, and laughed, sparkling with ancient water and immortality.

After they'd found their way back over the surface through the woods to where they started, at least one hundred yards away, they talked about the other place—"The Well," Wick wanted to call it. They vowed to keep it secret. So secret that soon they didn't speak of it, just sometimes, when anyone mentioned Old Crater or underground streams, exchanged a look, or not even a look, just shared consciousness.

But once was enough; they'd never done that dive again. Why risk what had been perfect?

***

In July, Wick told Tom he was ready. Sales were at a standstill, creditors closing in. He picked his evening. Nikki was off at camp in the mountains, and Elise was going to a gallery opening in the Arcade.

Wick's holding company owned the whole Old Crater tract, had bought it years ago. He'd spoken of donating it someday for a state recreation area, with a visitor center and walkways built down into the pit, but all he'd done was fence it and post signage to warn trespassers of danger. Tom watched Wick turn his Lexus onto the Old Crater dirt access road and park by the gate. Tom drove on along the state road in the car Wick had rented with his new identity. Wick had arranged another name and documents years back: he said it was a sensible thing for any businessman to do, and he'd taken care of it before means of identification got hard to obtain. On some level, Tom realized, Wick had always expected the business to collapse. He knew his Florida history of boom and bust.

Wick planned for his new identity to drive the car across the state tonight, get on a Fort Lauderdale late flight to the Bahamas, then fly on to where the money Wick had moved offshore was banked, a destination Wick said Tom was better off not knowing. Tucked beneath the passenger floor mat were the reservations and passport in a sealed envelope.

Tom parked the nondescript sedan in among pines that marked the spot they reckoned was as close as they could get to The Well. Wearing gloves and a Tyvek jumpsuit that came down over his new rubber boots, Tom took out his backpack and carryall and a long piece of rebar he'd laid across the back seat. He locked the car. He went through a break in the fence Wick had cut earlier in the summer—already rusting. Tom moved carefully through the woods to the hidden sinkhole. He pulled from his nylon carryall a small sledge and set to work.

Wick, he knew, had by now unlocked the padlock of the chain-link gate, gone through and pulled it to, and walked to Old Crater. Tom pictured him descending through clouds of midges. By the water, he'd leave his clothes, his keys, his cell phone, his big flashlight, and a partly drunk bottle of Jack Daniel's. Would Wick take one pull of the whiskey? Tom thought he would, while looking up, as Tom did, at the last color from the west touching the rippled clouds overhead. He'd put an underwater light around his head before he got into the water.

"The weak point of any faked death," Wick had said, "is the lack of a body. It has to go somewhere where it could plausibly disappear." Tom had asked why Wick couldn't just leave his evidence at Old Crater and walk over here, but Wick said, "No. They'll track me through the woods. It's conceivable they'll search with dogs. I have to go through the water, and come up where no one would expect. That's the beauty of it.

They'll think I'm stuck down there, somewhere in the depths of the sinkhole."

Tom tried to talk him out of it, one last chance, the day before, but Wick just said, "You think I can't do it? I've been practicing holding my breath for months."

Nearly 8:00. The sky above was losing light, shifting towards purple. Tom clicked on the camping lantern he'd brought. It caught the retinas of something in the shadows across—an owl, Tom thought, or a coon. Tom hung the lantern from a branch, aiming the beam down toward the water, to illuminate the spot and help Wick find it.

Elise, Wick had insisted, couldn't know. She had to act natural when he disappeared, and ignorance was the best guarantee of that. When it was all done, after a year, maybe, he'd secretly contact her, get her to come on what would look like a vacation to where he was living. She'd forgive the charade when she learned how much he'd rescued from the crash. Maybe he'd have started a new business on the island by then. Maybe she'd marry his new self, one day. And his daughter, they'd trust her with the secret at some point. Tom had listened to his romantic confidence, and said nothing.

Now Tom breathed in the humidity and heard the singing of mosquitoes. He tasted salt on his upper lip and knew he was sweating. What if Wick hadn't found the cave? The aquifer would be charged now, the water level higher in rainy season, the movement faster. On maps no stream was shown, but he and Wick understood what they had found years ago, the course of something, whether it reached the Little Peregrine or no. He waited.

He remembered the dim sense, when they moved through the darkness underwater, of other caverns opening to the side. Possibly Wick would turn somewhere and lose his way?

Perhaps Wick would simply not come up?

No, here he was, puffing, gasping, in the water, his headlamp a weak flicker. "Tom," he called softly. "Hey, y'there?"

Tom sat silent for a moment, then stirred. "Here, buddy, right here," he said.

"Can't find any foothold," Wick said. "Let down the rope."

"Mmmhmm," said Tom, "I'm doing it." He had the polypropylene mountaineering rope secured to the stake he'd driven deep into the ground, angled properly away, a couple of yards from the edge, something not part of Wick's original plan. Wick had wanted no marks anybody could find. But tying rope to some bush or sapling just wasn't secure enough for a full-grown man, and it would leave more trace, Tom had argued. A stake removed just left a single hole, sure to fill in with summer rain, and he assured Wick he'd put it under foliage where no one would look.

Tom clipped the rope to his climber's harness, and let himself down four feet, one boot propped on the side to keep him still. He could stretch his arms out and brush the sides of the hole with his gloves.

Wick, treading water, called out, "Hey, you didn't have to come down yourself. I could climb up."

A few feet lower and all Tom had to do was land on Wick's shoulders, paying out the rope, his weight pressing Wick down. He heard Wick's huff of surprise as he went under.

Wick reached to grasp Tom's legs but couldn't, his hands slipping off the slick jumpsuit. He flailed and ducked low, out from under Tom, but he couldn't wait long for air, and when he pushed his face up, three feet over, his headlamp showed his hand grasping for the edge. He coughed water out, and Tom was there, stepping down on his head, shoving him forward and under. Wick couldn't have grabbed more than half a breath. And Tom got back on his shoulders and held Wick down, his weight more than any upward force Wick could muster.

Would the drowned man have some bruises when he was found? What more natural, if he came up under some obstacle, in the cave, the underground river, the mineral subterranean world.

Wick had fallen forward and gone deeper.

Tom lifted his feet and went up a bit on the rope. Wick stayed down.

Tom waited, dangling. He flexed his hands and regripped the rope.

He imagined Wick trying to go back through the stream, against the flow, airless: no it was impossible.

The body surfaced, floating face down.

Tom waited, counting, making himself go slow.

When it had been five minutes, he pulled himself up. Once on the top, he lay there for a minute breathing, then stood, detached his line and coiled it up. He took the other rope he'd brought, regular twist, and tied it to the rebar stake, rope and metal both from Fenwick construction. He tossed the fresh line into the sink: it dangled against the side, just breaking the water, visibly unused. He looked down into the dark pool, at the back of a white water mammal, extinct. He pulled out a towel, and wiped his boots dry, then hung it around his neck. The lantern was starting to fade. It would die soon, no way to tell how early it had done so, whether Wick had made the simple error of not using fresh batteries, whether darkness kept Wick from finding the rope. From the backpack he took Wick's set of new casual clothes, and left them, the car keys tucked in the right shoe, near the stake. Tom put his harness, line, and sledge, into his backpack, and hoisted it. Not so heavy. Wick had planned for Tom to carry him out from here on his back, leaving no scent of Wick on the ground if dogs were used.

Tom walked out, following the path he'd taken before; this would have to look like the route Wick had come in when he set up the stake, rope, clothes, at some earlier time. Tom looked into the locked car. One corner of the envelope with the new identity's information poked out from underneath the floor mat, the way he'd left it.

Tom stayed in the shadows under the trees and moved parallel to the road till the car was out of view. He took off his boots and jumpsuit and put on his running shoes. The carryall was empty now. He rolled it up, and put it and the boots, the jumpsuit, and his gloves—only now did he remove them—into his backpack. He shouldered it, and stood square, in running shorts and t-shirt, running his hands through his sweat-soaked hair. He took a minute, thinking through the details, and left.

He walked. It was dark now, and he stayed just off the road, avoiding headlights. Brief rain pattered somewhere in the woods. He concentrated on keeping his mind empty, his pace, his breath, his heartbeat, even.

At the Spoonbill Shops, where he'd left his car, he slid the backpack inside a grocery bag on the floor, and went into the market. When he got home, he had two full grocery bags to carry inside. The sledge went into its slot among his tools. He hosed down his boots and jumpsuit and threw them, with rope and tackle, in the catamaran, among the rubble of his other outdoor gear, a temporary risk he'd have to take. He put his clothes in the washer, and stepped into the lap pool shower. Dressed in clean sweats, he started the wash, and went upstairs, unloaded groceries, and read for a while, or tried to. When he looked out at the golf course, he saw lightning flicker in the distance. He hoped it would rain a lot during the night.

A little after 11 the phone rang. He looked at the caller ID. After four rings, after the machine kicked in, he picked up, said, "Hello. Sorry, I was doing laundry."

Elise asked if he'd seen Wick that evening.

"No," he said, "I thought he was staying late in the office, paperwork."

"That's what he told me," she said, "but he isn't answering there, and his cell phone's off, and he hasn't come home."

"Maybe he's on the way. Or maybe he stopped off somewhere for a drink," said Tom.

"Maybe," she said. "I guess I'm silly to worry, but he's been odd lately."

"Under a lot of pressure," Tom said.

"Yes," she said. "Well. Sorry to bother you. I'll call the bar at the club—maybe he's there."

That conversation was on tape, if anybody ever got that far, checking.

***

In bad financial times, the state needed a good laugh. And Florida guffawed with scorn at the man who died faking his own death. Too tricky by half, that Bill "Wick" Fenwick, who thought he could thread his way under the surface, come up in a new spot, and get away. But no: after his wife's worried calls, police found his car parked by the gate to Old Crater. In the early morning light, it was easy to follow his track. There were his clothes, his wallet and keys still in his khakis, his cell phone on top of a little memo book, a note in there talking about how he'd always liked to come here to get close to nature, to get ideas. And now, in his despair, where could he turn for peace? (This was hokey, Tom thought, when he read it in the paper. No wonder Wick hadn't mentioned the note to him.) Further search turned up the other car, parked among pines, inside it the new identity, the planned escape. And from that end, they found the declivity with the rope dangling, and below it the body, a middle-aged man in swim trunks, with a lamp on his head, askew.

They brought in a diver who located the passage from sink-hole to sinkhole. It was assumed Wick had gotten through (a feat in itself, the sheriff said on TV), but didn't make it out of the deep water—no foothold and perhaps he couldn't find the rope in the dark, or couldn't climb it. Unnamed official sources were quoted speculating about how much whiskey he'd drunk, the lamp up above failing, maybe a cramp, maybe his heart, though it was found he'd definitely drowned. Anyway, it looked like justice.

Editorials said enough of these scoundrels.

Parents said sinkholes are very, very dangerous.

The widow and the daughter at the funeral were grateful for the support of old friends, of whom there were not many as the financial facts came out.

The businesses, layered with debt, would be closed in on by creditors. Forensic accountants found funds Wick had si-phoned overseas, though not as much as they hoped. Under Florida homestead law, business bankruptcy or not, the Mrs. got the house. Which she could sell, in time, when things had settled down.

The life insurance policy had long outlasted the suicide waiting period, and anyway it's not suicide if you die faking sui-cide, so, though there was comment about Wick's accident being the result of a planned embezzlement, in the end, she'd get that money, too.

Tom saw Elise at the funeral, and at the office a few times, only in public, all aboveboard. She looked pale, and spoke slowly, hesitantly, and people said she'd been given sedatives. And when she told friends she was taking Nikki away for a time, up to the mountains, people said, of course, poor thing, she's near a break-down, imagine the betrayal and bad publicity. But Tom was sure she was alert, and careful. Wick had underestimated her, Tom knew. She was an excellent actress.

She had told him, when he revealed Wick's plan to her in June, that she'd long suspected he'd do some such stupid thing, had seen the other ID in Wick's desk back when she found the private eye report. From then on she'd set aside cash culled from their expensive life and hidden it where it wouldn't be found, against the day when he abandoned her and Nikki.

Still, the details of Wick's plan had infuriated her. She said it was all boy's adventure and would look fishy, there'd be a lot of noise and a big chase after him, and then she'd be tied up in it, suspected. And when Wick was, inevitably, caught, and tried, and jailed, what a disaster for Nikki. Better he should fail, she said, and Tom had agreed.

***

At times Tom walked through waves of vertigo, a feeling that the ground beneath him could turn to powder, but he did what was demanded. He worked with the receivers, his employment now to salvage what could be saved. He got to know the accountants, who listened to his requests for payments that would keep things going and bring in revenue for a smaller, steadier business that could perhaps emerge in time.

In separate trips through August and September he'd dropped the rope, sledge, cut-up jumpsuit, each glove, each boot in the Little Peregrine, in distant spots, where the water ran fast and deep after tropical rains. Nobody was looking for them. Nobody was looking at him. The accountants talked about what Wick's books told them, about the nested companies making each other loans. Some days, they laughed and whistled with admiration at Wick's nerve.

In mid-November, Elise flew down from the mountains to come to the office to sign papers. She looked serious, and older, in a brown suit, no earrings, with a thread of gray in her hair. She said goodbye to him in front of others, saying to him, as to them all, "I hope we'll meet again."

But he knew it would be better not to. While she could visit here, and he could court her, even after a few years they could marry—that's how Wick would think—it was better for her to be free, and far away. He shook her hand, and wished her well.

Tom realized, of course, that she'd known in any plan Wick would turn to him, and so she'd made sure he was her ally. But once she was gone, he started thinking she must have seen, for a long time—years?—what he was capable of. Tom wondered exactly when he'd started hating Wick.

Playing the front nine one morning in early December, on a day when the humidity had cleared, he drove into a bunker. Stood there, waggling the five iron, feeling the sun on his bunched shoulders, the golden force of it. He swung and sprayed sand, and the ball lifted and reached the green, but there was nobody to see it. Then he got what he had lost. And what he had: his own shadow stretched unrivaled across the fairway.

Cave of the Winds

Azalea, Barry, Caterina, Darryl—three Tropical Storms and a Category One—formed off Africa in July and meandered into the North Atlantic without harming anyone, but their arrival started up the jitters.

Bad seasons had worried Carlos ever since two years back when Hurricane Allen grazed his neighborhood, and, even though it only knocked down some overgrown trees, Carlos knew they were vulnerable, with his and Jen's house only nine feet above sea level and six blocks from Biscayne Bay, so he decided to go take a look at one of the warehouse spaces his buddy Bernard had told him about, where, that particular summer evening, other guys who'd rented were scrubbing and painting and sharing beer out of battery-powered mini-fridges.

Caves of metal, they looked like from outside, each unit with a roll up/pull down door and a small conventional door beside it, each with a toilet/sink area that could be wallboarded off, and a shower added if you wanted, because that was the deal, you signed on for a year and you could fix the place up, make it better than the other strip warehouses in this area of Tangerine Gardens, which had no visible citrus trees nor gardens but was an unincorporated district, inland enough not to be in an evacuation zone, hot and ugly enough to be inexpensive, with elevation enough to stay dry unless there were a seven-mile storm surge.

Dave the realtor said that, after Dr. Sean McFadden, the meteorologist on TV, predicted there'd be five major storms this year, he'd gotten the idea to develop this as a rental shelter, with the two buildings facing each other, six units each, forming a good space in-between for parking and cooking out, and plenty of room per unit for a family, plus—Dave nodded knowingly—the other people who would be begging to be included.

"Everyone should be prepared to evacuate," had long been the advice, but recent seasons had demonstrated that getting up the state by car was not feasible, Florida being at least two tankfuls long and longer when everybody was idling in refugee backups on the turnpike until the stations ran out of gas with no restocking possible, so the new official wisdom said you should just go inland a bit and hunker, Bernard said, and Carlos put money down to lease a place beside Bernard's in the south building, which cost only a bit more, really, than a storage unit that size, so if it didn't work out, he'd use the space to hold the Deco sinks and lighting fixtures he pulled from old houses and, eventually, put into others he was restoring.

For each person, one gallon of clean drinking water per day for an estimated two weeks should be stockpiled, which for himself, Jen, and their eight year old, Riley, would be 42 gallons, but of course Jen would want to include her father, Big Riley, who had retired to the Keys and would be evacuating to join them, and, think of it, wouldn't water be a form of barter in the aftermath, so he just grabbed a couple of gallons each time he went through Publix, since bit by bit you don't notice the expense.

Generators need gas, but piling the unit with gallon cans of fuel was asking for trouble, and gas ages badly, its properties breaking down, according to what the small intense dentist who had the unit east of his said at a meeting where they all discussed whether it might be better to put in one big tank and arrange for delivery or accumulate empty cans to take to a nearby station to fill if a big storm threatened, and guys had theories one way or the other, but they listened to Carlos when he talked, because, from his work, he knew a few things about structural engineering and the horrors of getting permits.

He couldn't stay away on weekends, and then he started stopping in a couple of nights a week.

If he didn't go, he imagined others bringing in some new comfort like the queen-sized airbed with backrest and built-in pump he was considering buying from a catalog that the dentist, Mike, had told him about, and there had lately been talk about a bunch of them going to the shooting range that was in a warehouse a couple of blocks over, and perhaps even an excursion to a gun show, where George from the north building said you could buy hard-to-get guns no questions asked, although Carlos already had a permit for his pistol.

Jen complained that he was gone all the time and that he wasn't really present when he was home.

Kerosene lanterns, he wrote, *kerosene   extra wicks   propane grill   ¿ventilation fans?   instant coffee   powdered milk   sardines   crackers   duct tape   small saw   iodine   bandages   ¿pump action shotgun?   new gloves, 2 pairs*

"Listen," Jen said, "I don't understand why you are worrying like this when you know that if a storm comes, we'll stay here if it's just a Category One, or we'll leave if we have to, what's important is that we're all— are you listening to me?— what's wrong with you?— if you walk out now— please don't—"

Men need to take care of the family, didn't she understand that, he thought, sitting on a plastic lawn chair, watching Atlanta at Milwaukee on battery TV with Bernard (who was, as he often said, happily divorced) till it was time for the 11 p.m. advisory when Dr. Sean McFadden analyzed Tropical Storm Erin's eyewall development, and Mike the dentist, who had made mojitos at the wet bar he'd put in, showed them a book on paleo-tempestology, the study of ancient storm patterns, and Bernard remarked how many ancient cultures had a god of the wind, which led Carlos to mention El Nuberu, who was Asturian—the aunt who raised him told him that though they were Chilean their ancestors were from Asturia and that El Nuberu, if he were angry, could send a rain of frogs—and then Bernard found a list on-line of wind gods, Fujin, Vayu, Ehecatl the Aztec one, and the Incan, Kon, and they joked about naming this place the Kon-dominium, a refuge dedicated to a healthy respect for the deities of destruction, and when Carlos got home Jen was asleep and he crashed on the Florida room futon.

Nicaragua took a hit mid-August from Tropical Storm Fred (Erin had boiled up and broken on the mountains of Dominica), and Hurricane Gertrude drenched Belize two weeks later and headed into the Gulf towards Pensacola, and Dave brought in more renters, among them a guy named Dougie Poppelier who took the unit west of Bernard's, and Labor Day Weekend he and his girlfriend smoked pot in his unit, which everyone could tell, such was the ventilation, and then all through September, things were quiet in the Atlantic, just little "invests," as they called them on the Internet weather sites, seeds of possible storms that at most swirled up, lasted long enough to grab a name, then went nowhere, bringing a lot of talk about ocean temperatures at different depths.

October, though, brought Logan, strengthening fast and approaching eastern Cuba, with notice given for all tourists to leave the Keys, the first step in the evacuation process, and most models showed them in the cone of possibility, so the guys decided they would fuel up and do a test of the two big generators they'd all gone in on, one for each building, as Carlos had recommended.

"Power off," Dave shouted, and the building held its breath.

Quiet stretched until they heard the snort and roar, and along the heavy-duty cords they'd run through to each unit the juice powered up fans and fridges and Bernard's new red espresso machine.

Restrengthening after being smacked around by Cuba's mountains, reports from reconnaissance flights said, and now an evacuation order had gone out for Keys residents to leave, lower Keys first, starting at daybreak tomorrow, and then, perhaps Monday, they would issue an order for the Dade beaches, and if Logan looked like a Cat. Two, they'd call for everyone to leave the neighborhoods by the bay, not at all a sure thing, but Carlos got Jen to come over and see, telling her that way she could figure out what was missing, what they'd need to bring when they came for real in a couple of days.

Smoke rose into the pink evening sky as Jen mingled with the other women around the half drum grills, and Mike had made a big batch of Palomas, margaritas with grapefruit juice instead of lime, and Riley rode on his father's shoulders—almost too big now, his sandals digging into Carlos's ribs, so, Carlos thought, he's old enough to remember this, always—while they shared a Columbian-style arepa, fried corncakes filled with sweet cheese, not on Carlos's diet since the doctor started measuring his triglycerides, but in emergencies you need your strength, he told his son, and Riley wiped his hands on Carlos's hair, making it greasy and thick.

Time to prepare but not panic, Dr. Sean McFadden said in the 11 p.m. report, and the good news was Logan had taken a jog to the east, but the storm could still jog back so don't relax yet, and at that the men nodded and the party progressed, with music and Jen's pineapple cake and the sharing of private stocks of aged tequila and añejo rums, while Riley curled up on his sleeping bag, and Jen sniffed in the direction of Poppelier's place, but a couple of the new guys in the north building were cops and they weren't reacting so what business was it of hers, and in the end he did get her to test out the inflatable bed where they spent the night, though in the morning she insisted on going home early to shower, well before it would be time for Riley's school and her job, because he'd forgotten about her particular shampoo and detangler.

Unpredictably, Logan slowed, stalled, shifted east northeast, and weakened to barely a Category One, till it was clear they were only going to get the outer bands, equivalent to your normal South Florida tropical depression, but Jen had said things over the past couple of days like *"After the season was he planning to put all that junk in their house?"* and *"Didn't he know she had never really liked camping?"* and *"Did he really imagine that all those guys with girlfriends weren't married?"* so after work he joined the others going to the gun range, with its smells of warm metal and cosmoline and everyone wearing ear protectors, which gave them all a jolly robot look, and as he priced ammo he thought about how she seemed immune, not feeling the immensity of the world's powers the way he did, and he stepped outside and called her to say that with gusts to 35 miles per hour he might stay at the Kondo overnight, and then returned to shoot beside Mike the dentist, who understood what it was to respect the arbitrary.

Violin or flute, Carlos debated, as Logan's gusts produced a high-pitched elongated note overhead which he'd have to investigate in the morning, perhaps some strand of wire or a hole in a downspout being played, and as he lay on the mattress listening he remembered his aunt saying El Nuberu whistled up the winds in his cave and sent them across the sky, so he imagined air being slowly siphoned out of the room, and he tried to concentrate on the slow rise and fall of his chest till there came a sharp knock on the door, which he opened to find Jen with an overnight case, explaining that since her dad, still up from the Keys evacuation, was staying with Riley, she'd come over, and he said he thought she didn't like the place, and she said, "I thought you might be having a private party," and he said, "You mean with a woman?" and she said, "The thought occurred," and he, pleased, said, "I haven't seen one as cute as you, Jenny," which led her to lie down beside him, and when he said he thought she didn't like camping she replied, "But slumber parties, yes," and whether this proved she was braver than him or just as anxious but with different concerns, anyway, after a while the sound stopped bothering him and he slept.

When he went up on the roof, the next day, he found a puckered, rusted seam between his place and Bernard's, and the following weekend the two of them patched it, talking about how, in the winter, they might find an old car or boat to restore here, something that you could keep inside the unit, telling each other that, no matter what, having this space wasn't a bad deal, good to hang onto, no mistake.

Xavier and Yolanda can never be hurricane names, because X, Y, and Z are skipped, though if there were storms enough in one season, Alpha, Beta, Gamma, Delta and so on would be used, but they were still awaiting a Ramona in mid-November when George, who had gone hunting up by Ocala, brought back, packed in ice in his 4x4, a buck which he carved in the open space, using his chain saw and knives, and, though he shared out the venison, there were complaints about the lingering smell of blood and bone in the courtyard, and then, the electric bills higher than they should be, the cops figured out that Poppelier had some hydroponics action going on and raided him, having clarified first that no one else's unit would be compromised, but

Poppelier was long gone, just some grow lights left behind, so Bernard surmised that a cop had tipped him off, not wanting, after all, for there to be a trial where the defense might subpoena any of the girlfriends.

"Y is the secret," Mike the dentist said while hammering ice wrapped in a towel, "of manhood, the chromosome we have and women don't, the sex determinant, and it's specialized, with only 86 working genes while the X has over a thousand, from what I've been reading in this book about Y-chromosomal Adam, the father of all of us human men," and he put crushed ice into a tall pitcher and proceeded with the recipe he'd found online for this party they'd decided to have, guys-only, to celebrate the hurricane season's official end on the last night of November.

Zephyr cocktails had brandy, orange Curaçao, pineapple juice, maraschino liqueur, and Angostura bitters, and after Mike strained the mixture into martini glasses coated inside with lemon juice, everybody lifted a toast to welcome the gentler winds of Florida winter, but after one round of the Zephyr's boozy sweetness they switched to beer while discussing how much more lethal Zombies would have been, and they all settled outside, talking about how the season had been rough on other places, Nicaragua and Dominica and Pensacola and Belize, and then they fell silent, and Carlos noticed that he, like the others, leaned back and looked up into the plum-colored, deep, unreadable sky, because they knew having been spared for now just meant they were that much closer to their turn.

Texaco on Biscayne

After a group of us met for a girls' night out to see a movie, we were tempted over to the nearby not very good place for a drink and fried food and a table outside on a mild Miami January night. We split up in the parking lot. It was near midnight, and people stood outside by their cars, smoking and talking in the soft, humid air. My friend Jill had come with me, but two of the others lived closer to her, so she went home with them. If I'd driven her, maybe this wouldn't have happened. Or it would have, but we'd have been together and so everything would have been different.

I was heading home by myself, down Biscayne, when I felt the left rear tire go wrong and at the same time saw a guy driving along next to me gesturing at me to pull over. Had I hit something on the road, or did someone—this guy?—gash my tire at the restaurant? Was he predator or friend?

I was in a dark stretch of Biscayne, with residential neighborhoods off to each side behind walls and dark office towers and banks along the road. I could feel the tire deflating slowly, the car moving more and more unevenly, but I didn't want to stop here, even if I was going to stay locked in and phone someone. I remembered that another few minutes south there was a Texaco with a 24-hour FoodMart, so I lolloped along, heading there.

The guy beside me honked and waved, but I ignored him. He got behind me, and when I signaled to go left he did, too—but as I turned into the well-lit Texaco, he pulled away. For all I know, he was a Samaritan. I rolled to a stop at the side of the station, near the closed service bay, and ostentatiously pulled out my cell phone. And then wondered who to call. I had broken up with my boyfriend Steve six weeks ago.

I'd bought my car used. It was a big old SUV (I used to move furniture a lot, what can I say?) and I had a vague idea that the spare sat suspended below the car, to be wound down with a gizmo you assembled from rods stowed underneath the front seat somewhere. It was a pain. I could theoretically do this myself, but it was late at night, I was in nice clothes and stupid shoes, and I never felt I could tighten the lug nuts well enough.

Or I could leave the car here and have them deal with it in the morning, and call a cab. This seemed more sensible. The car would be safe enough here, wouldn't it? It wasn't going anywhere. But I should ask permission. I put my phone into my purse, which I clamped firmly under my arm, and got out to go into the FoodMart.

A man came out of nowhere in the dark and said, "You need a vacuum?"

I said, "No thank you."

He said, "Vacuum real good."

He was gap-toothed, genus crazy-homeless. I shook my head no and headed past him. He followed, praising the vacuum. I was unable to tell whether he wanted to sell me a vacuum or to use something at the station to vacuum my car.

He followed me into the FoodMart. Behind thick plastic, the cashier sat, a man of about 40, looking tired.

"Hello," I said, "I have a flat tire and I'd like to—"

"I do not speak English," he said, enunciating clearly.

Vacuum man stirred behind me. I glanced at him, then back at the cashier, who sat motionless.

"*Tengo problema con mi carro. Un* flat tire. *Quiero permission dejar mi carro aqui*," I said. What were the words for flat and tire?

In Spanish he said, "*You speak Spanish?*"

"*A little,*" I said. "*In high school I it studied. And here, in Miami, I have opportunity to speak it much times.*" I smiled.

Vacuum man had gone outside. I saw him hovering near the door. Waiting for me.

The cashier gazed at me sadly and said, "*From Argentina I came here. You can leave your car if you wish. Mine is proximate.*"

A man burst into the shop, hollering in rapid Spanish. I caught the word *police.* He kept pointing outside and I saw that a cab was now parked at the nearer pump. I tried to grasp the facts: He had a fare that was some kind of problem. The person wasn't paying or was drunk or obnoxious or sick, I wasn't sure, probably all of these. The cab driver had tried to eject him, he wouldn't go, and now the driver had called for help. I looked out but couldn't see the passenger in the dark interior of the cab. It was a saggy-looking vehicle, with the numbers of the company on the side.

I sidled over near the window and snuck my hand into my purse, again seeking my phone.

Vacuum man scuttled back inside the shop. "Beautiful vacuum," he said, and I contemplated the beautiful vacuum I'd like to be in.

I hunched my shoulder to block him and called Steve. Yes, we had broken up, but it wasn't nasty, and when you have been together for almost a year and then break up, isn't there some clause, good for a call in case of emergency, for six months or till either of you is officially established with someone else? Of course there is. He was asleep, but when I told him where I was and why, he said he was on his way.

The cabby had gone back out. He could be heard hollering in English at the customer that the police would be here soon and he should get the fuck out of the cab now.

The passenger replied, screaming defiant obscenities. The cabby stood by the pump, the passenger stayed inside.

In the shelter of the corner between window and cooler case, I fumbled in my purse for money and sorted out a few singles and put them in the pocket of my jacket: I wanted cash at hand, without having to open my pocketbook in front of anyone. I put my phone where I could find it fast. I was not one of those women with an organizer purse but I could see the point now. Having things in the right place could be life or death, in certain circumstances.

The battle of invective between the cab driver and the passenger went on. Through the door, Vacuum man watched them, and I noticed that he trembled. I became aware that there were other people watching. At the corner a couple of teenage boys stood under a massive streetlight. I imagined the boys lived somewhere nearby and were out for adventure, but who knew. They could be hustlers or drug dealers. And standing very still in the shadows to my left a skinny black man leaned against the wall of the shop with his hands in the pockets of his sweatshirt. I instantly regretted that I noticed he was black, and, looking closely, thought it was really his extreme thinness that worried me, as if he were famished.

A police cruiser pulled in with a chirp of the siren and swirled around to just behind the cab. Right after it, Steve drove in and parked behind my car. He got out and bent down to look at the flat tire. I left the FoodMart and walked straight to him, with my keys in my hand.

"I'm sorry," I said, "to bother you. I didn't know what else to do. It's too crazy here for me to change the tire myself"—he cut me a look—"even if I could. If you don't want to do it, leave it here and just drive me home."

He looked around at the onlookers and the cops huddled with the cab driver, and shook his head. "I wouldn't leave it here, Molly." He took the keys and opened the front door and found and started assembling the set of rods.

I thought of explaining that the dark compact beside my car was the manager's, but decided there should be no argument about anything, however trivial, when he was helping me.

We broke up because we had danced and re-danced what he wanted, what I wanted, who we each were, in a kind of figure eight of the good and the bad, until we were stalled. We just didn't know how to go forward. We hadn't exhausted desire. Right this minute, he looked good to me, not just because he was Galahad. Not just because he was cranking the spare out from underneath the car with an efficient, irascible perfection, the effort showing in his long legs. But partly because of that.

While he was under the car, Vacuum man edged towards me.

Steve stood up with the spare tire and said, "Molly, please go inside till I'm done with this." Then he said, "You're not dressed to be out here," looking me up and down, and I thought he thought I'd been on a date.

"I was out with the girls," I said.

"Mmmhmm," he said with a grin which meant, You women all dress up for each other but not for me. He opened up the back of my car to get the jack.

Vacuum man stayed with me as I walked toward the shop, and I said, "I really don't need a vacuum, but please take this," and handed him two dollars. He grabbed the cash and moved away.

When I got inside, I felt I should buy something. I chose a ginger ale, paying the cashier through the small opening in the plastic—it must be bulletproof plastic, I thought—then opened it and sipped. Cold gas burned my throat.

"*From Argentina you came here?*" I said.

He nodded. "*It is one year and ten months.*"

"*There have been hard times in Argentina I have heard. In the news on the radio. Problems with the money.*"

He said, "*Yes, there were terrible times, there, so bad that I had to leave my wife and two boys, to come here so they can eat.*" He began to speak more quickly, so I caught only phrases, but the meaning was clear enough, as he poured it out. *Financial conditions. Government mismanagement. Corruption. Stupidity. Debt. You can have worked and been honest and have a business, an honest business, and it all disappears. It is arbitrary. The money lost all value there, ridiculous inflation, all that you had worth nothing anymore. And then you must come here to this place just to feed your family.*

Outside, the police stood, one talking to the cab driver, the other to the passenger, their posture conveying the serious courtesy of the law. They were making progress. The passenger was out of the cab. One policeman was writing something down. I presumed the cabdriver wanted a record of this, in case the passenger at some later point complained. Steve had the car jacked up.

The cashier brought out pictures of his two boys: together, in some kind of uniform, perhaps of a Catholic school. They had their father's serious dark eyes. *"Do you have children?"* he asked.

"No," I said, and because I thought he would expect me to feel sad about this, I added, *"lamentablemente,"* although I had not been yearning for children and was generally annoyed by all the endless pressuring jabber about biological clocks and so on. And now I felt dragged into hypocrisy by my need to stay in the shop. And, after all, look at him, stuck here, trapped, because of those children, his hostages to fate.

The cab was gone. I didn't see where the passenger went; perhaps he had paid and was being driven home. The cops sat for a moment in their car, then pulled back onto Biscayne.

The watchers were out there: Vacuum man, the skinny black guy, the kids. Steve was working calmly, had the bad tire off, the other in position. No one, I noticed, went anywhere near him. This was the advantage of being a man, damn it.

The skinny black guy entered the shop, looked at me, nodded, and picked out a bottle of beer.

My Spanish was warming up, and I felt I should keep the conversation going, but I didn't want to ask the cashier what he thought of America. What could he think of it with this view every night? While the skinny black guy paid and left, I said, instead, *"I never visited Argentina, never went to—"* I started to say Latin America but South Florida is a Latin part of the Americas, surely, so I said, *"South America."*

"You should travel there," he said. *"You can use your Spanish there."*

"Argentina has much culture," I said.

"Beautiful architecture," he agreed, and he described some-place I couldn't completely follow—in Buenos Aires—a place with some kind of flowering trees or trees and flowers, *flores, arboles*— and the most *exquisito* something—something to eat?—and here we were in the fluorescent lit cube of a FoodMart, I thought, this awful exile and captivity. I wanted to bring up Borges. Would it be pretentious to bring up Borges? And then was it not true that Borges saw fate's circles and puzzles, the way any path of escape led back to destiny, which would make his seem to be not a momentary Argentinean problem but an absolute, and how would that cheer this man up?

Steve came in and said the spare was just meant to be a temporary substitute, so I'd need to get a real tire put on tomorrow. He'd follow me home, just in case the temp was no good.

"Could you tell what happened?" I said. "Did I hit something sharp? Or did somebody do something to the tire?"

"Too dark for me to see," he said. "Wherever you take it tomorrow they can do the tire autopsy."

I laughed. Tire autopsy. That was Steve: wry. I first liked him for his wryness.

I turned to the cashier and thanked him. *"I hope you well,"* I said. *"That things will get better."* I was full of goodwill and sentiment, suddenly. And relief.

He looked at me with weary tragedy and thanked me. He could not summon a smile.

Steve was out the door and on his way to his car.

As I left the shop, the skinny black guy lurched up to me, lifted his right hand, and said, "I bless you with the benediction of the soul. May the God of hope fill you with all joy and peace in believing, so that you may abound in hope. By the power of the Holy Spirit, Amen."

I thanked him and gave him a dollar. In my car, I put on the headlights and saw Vacuum man just around the corner of the building beside the repair bay, sitting on a canister vacuum cleaner, holding the beer the skinny black guy had bought.

I drove home, with Steve following me, and of course I invited him in. It was very late, and he had come when I called, a reliable man in a dangerous world. The kind of man, I now know, who would go far away to work if we needed it, our son and I. Not that we have needed it yet, but as I go along Biscayne sometimes with the baby in the car, I pass where the Texaco was. It was closed not long after that night, something to do with leaks from the underground tanks, and though they excavated, the holes were filled in with dirt and paved over and the station never reopened. Things got better in Argentina, and worse here, and I tell myself the clerk went home. Big signs now proclaim bargain rents in the office towers nearby. The FoodMart building, which sat empty for a time, was lately gutted and painted geranium pink to house a business selling flower pots and garden ornaments. Driving by, I look at their display of gauzy butterfly flags and think of all that can happen.